A MEAL TO DIE FOR

From the abundant antipasti of chicken-liver mousse, prosciutto-wrapped asparagus, grilled sardines, and other delicacies to the creamy delight of crawfish bisque, three types of pasta, and main entrées of roasted lamb, baked snapper, and chicken with artichokes and sausage, we are treated to flashbacks of Benny's life in a novel that blends the best of *Big Night* with *Goodfellas*.

"*A Meal to Die For* is deliciously sinful and fattening. Not since I read Rex Stout's *Too Many Cooks* while stuck on an Amtrak train have I been so entertained and famished at the same time. I hope Joseph Gannascoli and Allen C. Kupfer will dish up many more courses in the future."
—Loren Estleman, author of *Nicotine Kiss*

"Actor Gannascoli, best known for his role as Vito Spatafore on *The Sopranos*, with an assist from Kupfer (*The Journal of Professor Abraham Van Helsing*), serves up a solid debut filled with mouth-watering recipes. . . . The mix of haute cuisine and mafiosi is a natural—obviously Julia Child and Tony Soprano both like to eat, right? And how often do you see a mobster getting disrespect for 'revealing his limited knowledge of food and even more limited food choice experience'?"
—*Publishers Weekly*

A Meal to Die For

— A CULINARY NOVEL OF CRIME —

Joseph R. Gannascoli

WITH ALLEN C. KUPFER

A Tom Doherty Associates Book  New York

This is a work of fiction. All the characters and events portrayed in this novel are fictitious or are used fictitiously.

A MEAL TO DIE FOR: A CULINARY NOVEL OF CRIME

Copyright © 2006 by Joseph R. Gannascoli and The Literary Group International

Edited by Brian Thomsen

A Forge Book
Published by Tom Doherty Associates, LLC
175 Fifth Avenue
New York, NY 10010

www.tor.com

Forge® is a registered trademark of Tom Doherty Associates, LLC.

ISBN-13: 978-0-765-35314-6
ISBN-10: 0-765-35314-8

First Edition: January 2006
First Mass Market Edition: December 2006

Printed in the United States of America

0 9 8 7 6 5 4 3 2 1

Dedication and Acknowledgments

—

To my parents, Joe and Vivian,
for making me
to my sister, Susan, and brother-in-law, Bob
for supporting me
to my wife, Diana,
for understanding me
and me
for being me

I would also like to add special thanks to these restaurants
as they have all influenced me:

101
Angelo's
Areo
Brennan and Carr
Ciao Baby
Commander's Palace
Esca
Il Cortile
Joe's of Avenue U
Paneantico
Pastis
Patois Gravy Pacifico
Pearl Room
Piazza Mercato
Royal Crown

South Fin Marina Café
Uncle Bacala's
Water Zooi

—Joe

＞

For Karen Kupfer and James Kupfer, for always being there
For Carmela, my mom, for all the love

Thanks to Annie and Michael, my wonderful kids, for their love
and for tolerating their dad's strange enthusiasms; and thanks to
Patti Esposito, for support and love, and for being the wonderful
person she is. I'm also indebted to Justin Peckholdt for giving me
a lot of information on gambling. And thanks to all my friends,
past and present, from Brooklyn to the far end of Long Island.

And thanks to Joseph Gannascoli, actor, chef, and friend.

—Allen

＞

. . . and special thanks to Brian M. Thomsen and Frank Weimann
for their invaluable contribution to this book.

A Meal to Die For

"You know what's the whole problem with these young guys?"

"These punks!"

"Yeah."

"Yeah what?"

"The problem. It's always 'takeout.'"

"It's fast, it's easy. You have to agree."

"Yeah."

"You go in. Bam! It's in the bag. You come out. No time flat. And on to serious business."

"I know."

"It's not like there is always the time for a sit-down."

"I'm not saying that."

"So what are you saying?"

"It's not like the old days with Tommy Drambuie and Johnny Cashmire."

"So that's what you're saying?"

"I'm saying that these young guys don't know any better. The 'takeout' thing is not the only solution."

"Yeah, but it's their thing."

"Yeah."

"And as the low men on the totem pole, it's their responsibility."

"The way it should be."

"Always has been, always will."

"Yeah."

"And if the man upstairs doesn't mind . . ."

"Now wait a second. The man upstairs doesn't have a problem with the 'take-out' thing because he gets to do things by his own set of rules. I mean, it's not like he has to go hungry when things get rough."

"Yeah."

"Remember the time the man upstairs was upset about Marino's closing for that second honeymoon?"

"Yeah."

"Well, I had to do a drop-off there the next day, and lo and behold, what do I see? Marino stretched out on a table in the back, his linen shirt the color of marinara, with little chunks of meat all around. The place was a mess."

"The man was upset, so someone came up with a solution."

"Damn straight. Wall-eyed Willy told Marino that he better make some final arrangements before he left, and, bam bam, the next thing you know, Marino never makes that plane for the second honeymoon."

"What about his wife?"

"She was already there, and boy was she pissed!"

"No kidding."

"What could she expect? The man was up all night making a week's worth of marinara with meat sauce for the man upstairs. He was exhausted. Passed out in the kitchen right there."

"He finished the supply of sauce, though."

"Of course, he wasn't stupid. The man upstairs gets what the man upstairs wants."

"Damn straight."

"Marino did catch the next flight south on the following day."

"That's not all he caught. He caught his wife with a spic cabana boy

doing the indoor/outdoor plumbing in the honeymoon suite that Marino had already paid for."

"She didn't think he was coming."

"She made a big mistake."

"And how!"

"The cabana boy got his, too."

"You mean after he got caught getting his."

"Yeah."

"The man upstairs was happy to oblige. He knows it's the little things that count."

"I heard the man upstairs even sent a few broads down to Florida for Marino."

"What did his wife say about that?"

"The man's wife?"

"No, Marino's."

"No one asked her."

(Laughter)

"Hey, good marinara with meat sauce is hard to find."

"So back to my original point. Don't tell me the man upstairs is eating take-out."

"Never said he was."

"Gentlemen, your lunch is ready."

"And thank God neither are we."

"Thanks, Benny."

NYPD surveillance tape
Case # 59-87643

⟿ The Menu ⟿

Assorted Antipasti

Appetizer
Seared foie gras with roasted apricots & sour cherry syrup

Soup
Crawfish bisque
Escarole with white beans & prosciutto

Salad
Blood oranges & anchovies with pine nuts over Boston Bibb lettuce

---

Fish and Chicken
Baked snapper in sea-salt crust
Chicken with fresh artichokes & sausage

Pasta
Perciatelli with sardines, fennel greens, toasted bread crumbs
Rigatoni with shiitake mushrooms, smoked mozzarella, & arugula
Orecchiette with sausage & broccoli rabe pesto

Meat

Roasted lamb shanks with orzo, veal reduction, mirepoix, &
mascarpone
Various vegetables & starches

—

Coffee and Biscotti

French roast coffee
Decaf (if necessary)
Espresso

—

Sorbet

A choice of
Granny Smith apple
Coconut
Mango

—

Dessert

Tiramisu with cannoli cream

—

Cigars and Cordials

Antipasti

—

Chicken-liver mousse

Marinated bocconcini

Grilled sardines

Eggplant wrapped with goat cheese

Crabmeat & cheese fondue

Prosciutto-wrapped asparagus

Chorizo and mussels

Baked clams & oysters Rockefeller

Pancetta-wrapped shrimp

Carpaccio of diver sea scallops with ponzu sauce

Assorted breads

Assorted olives

Reggiano cheese chunks

⬥ Chicken-Liver Mousse ⬥

Sauté shallots and chicken livers in butter until cooked through.
Remove livers; splash with port wine.
Reduce and scrape bottom of pan.
Put in robot coupe; puree till smooth
Add heavy cream; strain through chinois.
Salt and pepper to taste.
Chill until served.

⬥ Marinated Bocconcini ⬥

Toss olive oil, oregano, red pepper flakes, julienne of basil, julienne of roasted peppers.

⬥ Grilled Sardines ⬥

Lay sardines in casserole pan.
Cover with extra-virgin olive oil, sliced garlic, juliennes of lemon zest.
Grill.

⬥ Eggplant Wrapped with Goat Cheese ⬥

Thinly slice eggplant; dip in beaten eggs; flour; fry.
Drain and set aside.
In a bowl, soften goat cheese.
Add mix of fresh herbs (oregano, basil, thyme).
Roll tablespoon of cheese into cigar shape.
Wrap with sliced eggplant.

⬥ Crabmeat & Cheese Fondue ⬥

Thoroughly clean crabmeat, removing all shell shards.
Heat fresh cream in double boiler.
Melt in fontina and Gruyère cheeses.
Fold in crabmeat.
Season with salt and pepper to taste.

➳ Prosciutto-Wrapped Asparagus ➳

Poach asparagus until bright green.
Shock in ice water.
Wrap stalks with sliced prosciutto.

➳ Chorizo and Mussels ➳

Sauté sliced chorizo in olive oil until brown.
Add mussels.
Splash with white wine and a ladle of tomato sauce.
Cool until mussels open.

➳ Baked Clams & Oysters Rockefeller ➳

Open clams; top with seasoned bread crumbs.
Open oysters.
In a separate pan, sauté shallots and butter until soft.
Add splash of Pernod.
Add heavy cream.
Thicken with roux.
Add chopped spinach and salt and pepper to taste.
Top oysters.
Bake.

➳ Pancetta-Wrapped Shrimp ➳

Slice pancetta.
Wrap each shrimp with a slice.
Bake until bacon crisps and shrimps are cooked through.

➳ Carpaccio of Diver Sea Scallops with Ponzu Sauce ➳

Slice scallops very thin.
Fan on a plate.
Pour ponzu (soy sauce with lemon juice) over scallops.
Top with thinly sliced jalapeños.

Prelude

Benny Lacoco walked across the street, pulled open the door to Cobbler's, a neighborhood bar, and shook off the cold. The odor of beer and spirits hit him, but it was the warmth of the place that he immediately sensed.

It was goddamned cold outside, and the evening sky was dark, but it had that velvety, cloudy grayness that often predicts an impending snowstorm.

Everything was quiet: the few people walking the streets, the traffic, everything.

In fact, it was too quiet.

Even for a Monday night.

Especially for Brooklyn.

More than anything, it was that stillness that made Benny nervous. It reminded him of a lot of old westerns he had watched on television. There was always that moment in those movies and television shows, when the two protagonists—usually the sheriff and the head outlaw—approached each other down Main Street, their hands dangling by their sides an inch or two from the revolvers in their worn, leather holsters, their eyes fixed intently on each other. Then they'd stop and there would be that totally silent, totally still second or two before they would draw their guns and fire at each other.

It was the eventual gunfire that audiences found satisfying. But it was that pause—that hellish, quiet second or two—that got on Benny's nerves. Shoot the bastard, he used to think. What the hell are you waiting for? Shoot, damn it!

Right now, as Cobbler's stained glass and steel door closed behind him, Benny felt like he was caught in a real-world suspension of time like the scenes in the old westerns. Only he knew this feeling wouldn't be over in a second or two. Probably not even an hour or two. Maybe if he were lucky it would be over before the early hours prior to daybreak, when he'd be meeting his friend Joey Arso back here in Cobbler's.

Yeah, lucky, Benny thought, pulling up a red-cushioned stool at one end of the bar. From this seat by the window facing the avenue he could keep an eye on the open but staffless restaurant he had just left.

He didn't know if he'd be lucky or not.

He didn't know shit.

"What can I do you for?" the bartender asked.

"Lemme have a Heineken," Benny said, reaching into his pocket and throwing a twenty-dollar bill on the bar.

"You got it!" the bartender replied. He was about thirty, several years younger than Benny himself, but he dressed like most of the clientele of the bar, who looked like they were in their early twenties.

Benny's thoughts turned back to the evening ahead of him.

Lucky! he thought. I'll be cooking all night and my reward could be a piece of lead in the head.

The bartender brought the beer, took the twenty, returned the change, and drifted back down to the far end of the bar, where he was engaged in entertaining two women trying hard to look twentyish.

Benny quickly checked out both of the women.

One had a nice shape, a decent profile, and a stylish haircut that circled and complemented her face. And she was wearing boots with stiletto heels that absolutely screamed "Fuck me!" She was provocatively sucking on a straw, all the time making eye contact with the bartender.

The other woman, Benny assessed, was a skank. Period.

However, Benny wasn't interested in women tonight, and that in itself was unusual. This was going to be a really strange, tense night, perhaps the most nerve-racking night in Benny's somewhat unconventional life.

And it was still early.

The night hadn't even really begun yet.

The Gunfight at Bay Ridge—if it were to occur—wouldn't be starting until the sumptuous meal Benny was preparing was reaching its end.

He sighed and said, "Shit." Then he downed half the Heineken and looked across the street to the front of the Il Bambino restaurant.

"Shit," he repeated, mumbling the word to himself. Benny was tired. He had been in the restaurant since one o'clock in the afternoon. And before that he had personally selected and paid for a lot of the food he'd been preparing all afternoon. He wasn't going to leave that to anyone else. After all, he had a reputation to keep. Nor was he going to use many of the supplies that Il Bambino stocked. The place was a decent enough neighborhood restaurant, but it never quite achieved greatness in anything: not in its recipes or the quality of its food, not in its ambience, not in its service. He was somewhat surprised when he got the call "from above" over the weekend instructing him to be at *this* restaurant on Monday night to prepare a meal for some of the family.

Face it, Il Bambino was no great shakes.

But someone at the top must have had his reasons. Maybe the owner owed a favor. Or, Benny thought, maybe it was the Bay Ridge neighborhood, which was usually quiet and unpopulated late in the evening on a Monday night, when most of the neighbors were home watching Monday night football on television.

Benny himself kept an eye on the television screens in Cobbler's. More than one of them was tuned in to Monday night football. Benny had a couple of hundred riding on a straight bet on the Giants game, and after the financial beating he had taken the day before, he was eager to make his money back. God knows, the three-team teaser he had had for Sunday's games had left him almost a grand and a half in the hole.

Those goddamn underdog Packers! They had fucked him over again.

Whatever.

He turned his thoughts back to the night ahead of him.

It wasn't his place to question. He got the call to show up tonight, and he was here.

He just had to do what he did best: prepare practically legendary meals. Meals to die for, some of the guys at the top had called them.

Benny shifted his two-hundred-and-fifty-pound frame on the

bar stool and drank down another mouthful of beer. He reached into his coat pocket and pulled out a box of Marlboro Lights, then remembered that he couldn't smoke in the bar. For a moment, he weighed his choices: go outside in the cold to smoke or just wait a while for the cigarette. Or he could just light up, but that might cause a minor scene, which was something he didn't want.

Not tonight.

A low profile was in order.

He opted to wait. It was just too nasty out there.

Goddamn stupid law, he thought. Can't smoke in a bar! What's this city coming to? Pretty soon you won't be able to *drink* in a fucking bar.

The bartender approached him again. "Get you another?"

"Yeah, okay," Benny answered. He had to kill some more time, at least until his "guests" showed up, not that he knew who all of them would be. As they showed up, he guessed that he would recognize some (maybe even all) of them, but right now he had little idea who had been summoned to this dinner. He didn't want to be in the restaurant as they arrived, because that would mean more time shooting the shit with a lot of them. And some of the likely invitees he couldn't stand. Some of the guys were straight-up; others were windbags or assholes. He'd rather sit in this bar for a while, at least until enough of the guys showed up so that they could amuse themselves.

He knew he'd have to make nice with all of them, whoever they turned out to be. A lot of them probably would have been connected far longer than he had and would technically have rank over him.

But Benny had an ace in the hole when it came to position in the family.

In the kitchen, Benny reigned supreme.

If the goombahs got overbearing, he could always withdraw to the kitchen, claiming he had to stir something, chop something, or keep an eye on something being prepared. And few would question him about it.

Besides, Benny didn't feel like talking much tonight. Because deep inside, he was nervous. Scared, even. Thank God, the preparation of the many courses of this meal would keep his mind preoccupied. It'd help get him through the night.

The bartender brought the beer and asked Benny if he was through with the first one. Benny drank down the last of it and handed the empty bottle to him. "Yeah, thanks."

The kid took another few dollars from the bar and rang it up on the register. Then the skanky chick called him back down to the other end of the bar again. The good-looking barkeep scooted down to her and her friend. Then she whispered something in his ear as she stroked his cheek with the tips of her fingers.

Jesus, go for the other one, the one in the boots, Benny thought. At least fucking her won't put sores on your dick.

Then, just as the juke box in the bar began blasting "Here I Go Again" by Whitesnake, a car pulled up outside Il Bambino. Benny didn't recognize the black Cadillac Seville, but he did recognize the man who got out of the passenger door. It was Palumbo. Thomas Palumbo. Or "Pally" as he was called by most of the soldiers. Benny always thought the name was ironic, because as far as he was concerned, Pally was one of the biggest pricks he had ever met. The men at the top seemed to love Pally because he was efficient, apparently loyal, and always got the job done, whatever his job *was*; not too many people seemed to be too clear what that was. But one thing was certain: if you were ever in a jam or needed a break or some help, you could never count on Pally Palumbo to cut you any slack. But he *would* "cut" you.

Palumbo entered the restaurant, but a minute later he was back outside, looking confused (probably because the restaurant was completely empty) and lighting a cigarette. Then he started to walk casually along Third Avenue. It was obvious to Benny that Pally didn't want to be the first to arrive . . . or sit down. (At least not in an empty restaurant.) So he walked, puffing on a butt. He was wearing a black overcoat over his short, weaselly body, and his shoes were so shiny Benny could see the streetlights reflecting off them from his vantage point across the street.

Seeing Pally smoke made Benny's desire for a cigarette grow, but he fought the urge. The last thing he wanted was to go outside, get noticed by Pally, and have to engage in small talk with the son of a bitch.

Fuck that!

Benny would rather go without the smoke.

Seemingly from out of nowhere, another of the guests was standing in front of the restaurant. Benny recognized him, too: it was Dominick "Aspirin" Aspromonte. His nickname *was* meant to be ironic. Aspirin made most of his money from drug trafficking. Many of the guys knew this; thus his nickname. But this part of his business dealings was never openly sanctioned by the family, and to some of the more senior members it was an embarrassment. Others, though, seemed to turn a blind eye to it.

Nonetheless, Aspromonte was responsible for more of the importation of heroin to this country from Asia than anyone else Benny knew about. Most of it was brought in in otherwise empty DVD cases from Shanghai, cases that supposedly had martial arts movies with titles like *Shaolin Assassin* or *Kung Fu from Beyond the*

Grave in them. Aspromonte once told Benny his motto was "No disc . . . and no risk!" So at least Aspromonte had a sense of humor, which wasn't always easy in the world in which he operated. Anyhow, a sense of humor was more than that scumbag Pally had.

Aspromonte spotted Pally and waved to him. Pally seemed to be trying to act casual, like he had just been leisurely arriving, and made a big show of approaching Aspromonte and shaking his hand. Benny noticed that the phony prick put on a big smile, shook Aspromonte's hand, and covered the outside of the hand with his other one, cupping it between them. Like Pally was *so* fucking glad to see him.

He'll be glad to cut your heart out at the first opportunity if it'll benefit him too, Benny thought. The fucking guy makes me sick.

Palumbo and Aspromonte went into the Il Bambino together. Benny thought about just lighting up that cigarette he was dying for in the bar but again decided against it. No one else in the place was smoking. Why cause a scene? It wasn't worth it . . . not here, not tonight. Instead, he decided the time might be right to sneak outside and have that smoke.

"I'll be right back," he yelled to the bartender, who nodded back at him. Benny stepped outside and a few steps up the block from the corner bar, away from the avenue. He lit up the cigarette with his Zippo and took a drag on the smoke, shooting glances behind him up the block and back toward the restaurant.

Two more men approached the restaurant on foot. One of them Benny recognized by looking at him. Michael Ischia's long black hair was his trademark and had been so since the 1960s. Benny had seen old pictures of him with his hair down around his shoulders, looking like a keyboard player from some old late-1960s psychedelic band. These days, Ischia's hairline had receded a bit, but what hair he still had was almost as long as it had been when Three Dog Night was cranking out new hit singles. Now it was thin and combed back and, Benny thought, most likely blackened with Grecian Formula.

Ischia was a strange guy with deep, dark, almost frightening eyes. Benny had never had many dealings with him, but on those occasions when they had met—someone's wedding or, more often, someone's funeral—he had seemed like an alright guy.

Benny recognized the other man he was with, but not from sight. Benny recognized his loud voice and obnoxious laugh. Matthew Di Pietro's laughter could drive anyone nuts. And he laughed all the time. Often, it seemed, for no reason. He was laughing when Benny spotted him. Loudly. But Ischia wasn't laughing; he was grinning, not laughing. He was probably just humoring his associate.

Benny ducked between two parked cars to avoid being seen by the pair. He still wasn't ready to go back to the restaurant, though he knew he'd have to go back soon.

Finally, the two went inside Il Bambino. Di Pietro! Benny thought. Jeez, I'll poison the fuck if I have to listen to his cackling all night. Di Pietro fancied himself a social butterfly. He managed a Brooklyn heavy-metal rock club nestled in a Bensonhurst warehouse (even though he dressed and looked more like Paul Anka than Ozzy Osbourne). Benny found it amazing how such an annoying guy could be so successful, but he had to give Di Pietro credit. The guy had kept the place open since the 1980s, it was still thriving even now, and it brought in a fortune. And it gave some of the higher-ups' kids—those who fancied themselves future rock stars—a venue to showcase their bands, often as opening acts for second-string but nonetheless nationally known heavy-metal bands.

As far as Ischia, Benny was never quite sure what the guy's function was within the organization. He still didn't know. Sometimes it was better *not* to know, not to even ask. If he needed to know, Ischia himself or someone else would tell him.

Benny tossed the butt into the street and went back in the bar. The bartender noticed the red color on Benny's face.

"Cold as a witch's twat out there, huh?" he commented.

Benny nodded, then drained the Heineken. He pushed the remaining singles on the bar toward the kid.

"Thanks," Benny said. "Keep it."

Then he stepped outside into the cold again and looked at his watch. Ten forty-two.

Better get back to work, he thought. Lots to do. This meal *has* to be one these guys won't forget. And one that one guy won't remember . . . because he probably wouldn't be alive at the end of the night.

Benny crossed Third Avenue, but as he reached the opposite curb he noticed an apple red Audi convertible pulling up behind him. It slowed to a crawl when it reached him. Its top was open and from inside he heard the words "Hey jack-off! How come you ain't in the kitchen?"

Benny turned, looked at the driver, and responded, "Because I'm out here talking to a convertible-driving, ugly-looking pansy asshole like you."

Then both men smiled, and Benny reached into the Audi and vigorously shook the man's hand. It was Anthony "Double A" Abbazio, a friend he had known since his freshman year of high school.

Abbazio's smile disappeared in a flash. Throwing the Audi into neutral, he said, "Hey, Benny, no kidding around. You got any idea what this meeting tonight is all about?"

Benny noted his friend's seriousness. "It has to have something to do with the capo's trial, wouldn't you say?"

"I guess." Abbazio looked away from Benny, then added, "But I don't mind tellin' you I don't like the look of it."

Benny said, "I gotta tell you I'm a bit . . . nervous. If you know what I mean."

"Yeah. I know. Me too. To put it mildly."

"Listen," Benny went on, "you got a, shall we say, guilty conscience? Man to man, friend to friend."

Abbazio exhaled deeply. "I mean . . . shit, Benny . . . don't we all? In one way or another?"

Benny wasn't sure how to answer, but he did anyway. "Yeah, I guess so."

Then there was a moment of silence. Neither man would look at the other. Neither knew if they would ever see the other again after this night. They liked the other; both had had good times together. But there was only so far this conversation could go, even with the long-term bonds of friendship between them.

Benny broke the awkward silence. "You better go park that imported piece of shit, and I better get back to work in the kitchen. Some of the guys are already inside, probably wondering where the fuck I am."

"Yeah," his friend replied. "But make this meal extra special, man, you know, just in case."

Benny picked up on the undercurrent of that remark but tried to change the mood. "All my meals are extra special, you know that."

Abbazio's demeanor changed again. Keeping his foot on the brake, he shifted the car into drive and said, "One more thing. Go fuck yourself, Benny."

Benny laughed as Abbazio turned the corner. The son of a bitch had been telling him "go fuck yourself" since their days as St. Dominic's High School. Over the years it had become his friend's standard way to say "good-bye," almost a term of affection.

For a moment, Benny stared after him. God, the trouble they used to get into in high school!

Then he snapped out of the reverie. He whispered the word "shit" and unlocked the side door of the restaurant with a key that had been given to him.

The kitchen of this place was no great shakes—it was smaller and not as well equipped as any of the finer, upper echelon ones he had worked in recently—but it was good enough for him to prepare a meal the likes of which none of the guys present would ever forget.

Once inside, he hung up his coat and looked around. He had been preparing the food most of the day, and he was tired, but the night was really just about to begin. He was confident that there'd be absolutely no complaints about his cuisine; his meals were legendary throughout the tristate area, and whenever the bosses from out of town were in New York on business, Benny's place, Pazzo Oeuf, was where they came to eat—or wherever he happened to be working on special occasions. Benny had never heard any complaints from any of these guests unless it was some soldier unfavorably comparing Benny's entrée to something the soldier's dear old mother cooked a certain way. But those comments were more sentimentality than complaint, and neither Benny nor anyone else ever took them very seriously.

On the other hand, Benny's artistry with food had helped him along in his careers—culinary and otherwise. Often, one of his "specials," one of his finest kitchen creations, had literally saved his ass. He had found that the way to someone who's about to cut you a new asshole's heart *was* through his stomach. Great food *could* mellow a guy out even if the guy didn't really appreciate what he was eating or the amount of creativity or skill that had gone into the dish. He had seen that happen again and again.

Not to mention what food could do to a chick's attitude toward you.

His mind suddenly turned to Teena. She was some girl. But that was a long time ago.

Teena!

Shit!

He forced his thoughts away from her. This was not the time. That was *long* over. And there was still plenty of work to do. Gotta stay focused.

Benny heard a commotion out front in the dining room. He peered out through a little window and saw Anthony Abbazio shaking hands with the guys who were already seated or standing by the bar. Abbazio had apparently run into a couple of other guys outside, and they were loudly greeting the rest of the company too.

Salvatore Sapienza was one of them.

Benny didn't know much about the big guy. He just knew that he was one tough son of a bitch. He stood about six foot three and had the biggest arms and shoulders Benny had ever seen on a guy who wasn't really a world-class weight lifter. Sapienza was the last guy you'd want threatening to use muscle on you because this guy literally *had* muscle—plenty of it, too. He was also a student of the martial arts, something he had been into, Benny had heard, long before the rush of kung fu movies in the 1970s and 1980s, when everybody and his grandmother was taking classes in tae kwon do.

Perhaps fittingly, Sap—Benny would never call him that to his face, although that was the nickname some of the higher-ups had given him—was a real sportsman. He had been working the gambling rackets for years with a great deal of success. Anyone's worst nightmare would be Sapienza holding you by the front of your shirt, his beefy fist in your face, asking you for the five or ten grand you owed him.

Oddly, Sapienza was a funny guy with a big sense of humor. It was easy to make him laugh, which lots of the guys tried to do because it would make *them* laugh, too. Sap's laugh sounded like something halfway between a throaty woman and a horse. When he let out a big laugh, it was hard not to laugh with him . . . or at him.

The guys were shaking hands, making small talk, patting each other on the back, and kissing each other on the cheek. Ischia yelled out over the noise, "Hey, I'm thirsty. Who wants to play bartender?"

Aspromonte responded, "Well, since you brought it up, why don't you, Mike?"

Before Ischia had time to answer, Palumbo raised his arms to quiet everybody down. "Hey, shush up. I got a question. Who's running this shindig?"

A silence fell over the assembled guests. Benny stared through a small square window from which he could see the dining room. He couldn't believe that Pally could be such a schmuck. If there was one thing that all the guys *did* know about this dinner meeting, it was that someone at the top had called it and was therefore "running" it. And you didn't question. You just didn't. You just showed up, as ordered.

Pally noticed the looks on most of the guys' faces. "What the fuck is the matter with all of you? You know who's in charge, just the same as I do."

Di Pietro asked, "Yeah? Who?"

Pally shook his head. "Who do you think? Who's serving us this meal? Who's in the kitchen right now cooking? Fuckin' Benny Lacocco, that's who."

Many of the guys' facial expressions changed to looks of relief. Most of the tension in the muscles on their faces seemed to just melt away. Benny felt better too, although he thought he knew what was coming next.

Palumbo walked to the entrance door of the kitchen and pushed it open but didn't go in. Even *he* knew that to Benny a kitchen was like a church and Benny was the monsignor.

"Benny, you lazy bastard, get out here and fix us some drinks," Palumbo ordered.

Aspromonte shot a glance at Abbazio. The latter could read it. It said, "There's gonna be trouble." The rest of the guys stood still. They knew something was about to go down too.

Fucking Pally, Benny thought. Always the asshole. Calmly, he put down the knife he was using and walked to the door still being held open by Palumbo.

When Benny stepped into the dining room, the rest of the guys applauded, yelling, "Bravo!"

Ischia bowed in Benny's direction and said, "Gentlemen, I give you the King of the Kitchen! Benny Lacoco!"

All of the guys continued to applaud. All except Pally, who stood by the door, smirking.

Benny raised his arms and said jovially, "Thank you, thank you one and . . ." Then he looked straight at Palumbo ". . . almost all."

The guys laughed. Again, all except Pally, who obviously didn't like the fact that Benny had wised off back at him.

"You gonna serve us drinks, King?" Pally asked, sarcastically dragging out the word "king."

Benny didn't really want to get into a pissing contest with Palumbo, so he addressed all the guys. "Let me ask you guys something? Any of you think you can prepare a feast the way I can?"

Some of the guests shook their head. Others just sat still.

"Any of you know what you're doing in a kitchen?"

"Shit, no," Apromonte said aloud. "I can hardly open a fuckin' can of anchovies!"

Some of the guys laughed. Benny smiled.

"But all you guys know how to pour a drink, don't you?"

He turned to Pally and said, "So I can't be two places at once. Elect yourselves a bartender."

Pally's face reddened. He must have thought that Benny was "electing" him to serve the drinks, and he was pissed off.

Abbazio picked up on this, and in order to spare his pal Benny any further grief—maybe even trouble that could get back to the bosses—he stood up and announced, "Hey, I volunteer. I won't even water down the drinks."

Benny nodded at his friend. "Thanks. Then I'll get back to work."

Then, ignoring Pally completely, Benny returned to the kitchen, letting the door practically swing shut in Pally's face.

"Fucking guy can't take a joke," Pally said to his cohorts. He ran his fingers through his graying hair. "Anyhow, Double A, I'll have a Dewar's on the rocks. In fact, why don't you make it a double?"

Abbazio eased himself behind the bar. "You got it."

The rest of the guys drifted over toward the bar.

Back in the kitchen, Benny turned his attention to the bread he was toasting, but couldn't get Pally off his mind. Motherfucking blowhard, he thought. I'd pray he'd choke on his food except that would be wasting too good a meal on him.

Then he thought that maybe there was someone—or several people—at the top who felt similarly about Palumbo. Maybe this whole get-together was going to be a "surprise party" for Pally. Maybe Pally had something to do with the capo's troubles. That would be justice.

Then again, Benny reflected, less happily, it might be my last supper, though he couldn't think of any great offense he might have committed against any of the higher-ups.

Christ!

Benny placed a couple more slices of bread onto the grill.

Two more guys walked into the restaurant. One puffed on a cigar. Before he even had his coat off, he said, "We can smoke in here, right?"

"Go ahead, Guy," Sapienza said. "We got the place to ourselves tonight. Smoke your lungs out."

Gaetano Ianello blew a long cloud of smoke. "That's just what I'll do. Thanks."

Ianello was a total mystery to Benny. Of course, he had seen him around at various functions, but Benny had never really spoken to him at any great length or ever had any dealings with him.

He was easily the oldest man at the dinner tonight, and he exuded an air of true confidence that the other guys didn't have. Benny thought to himself that if there were one true "made" man there that night, Ianello was the guy who fit the bill.

At least he *looked* like he did.

Benny recognized the fellow with Ianello. It was Joseph Garguilo. Garguilo was always a "shining star" in the family, unlike Ianello, who had had several close calls with a Queens branch of the family.

Benny always thought of Garguilo as a "chef," too. But his specialties weren't of the culinary variety. Garguilo was a family accountant: he cooked the books. Benny had known Garguilo since high school days, although they had gone to different, often competing, Catholic schools. Garguilo's days at Xavier High School were legendary. He had to hold the metropolitan area's record for a sixteen-year-old selling grass. Kids from every local school would seek Benny out in Owl's Head Park on Sixty-seventh Street. That was where he had his "office," which consisted of a concrete-and-wood park bench and a concrete table with a built-in checkerboard.

Benny remembered his first car, a bright yellow Volkswagen Beetle (hardly a pussy magnet). Then he remembered Garguilo's car at the time: a totally souped-up, gleaming green 1970 GTO. Obviously, Garguilo's bookkeeping—not to mention importing and sales—skills were in full swing even back then.

"So when do we eat?" asked Ianello, throwing his Brooks Brothers overcoat onto a table.

"Benny's working on it," Aspromonte replied from behind the bar, where he seemed completely comfortable. "The bar's open. What'll you have?"

"Gimme a Bloody Mary."

Then, just as Aspromonte was about to pour some Grey Goose vodka into a glass, Garguilo added, "Same for me. Just hold the vodka and the tomato juice. Just give me Mary. I could use a blow job."

Sapienza let out his horse laugh, and many of the other guys cackled too. Whether they were laughing at Garguilo's "joke" or laughing at the loud, raspy sounds emitting from Sapienza's lungs Benny couldn't figure out.

Ianello slapped the mahogany surface of the bar. "I'll still have it with the alcohol in it. I can get a blow job later."

Benny checked on the apricots he was roasting. Blow job? he wondered. He thought the odds were fifty-fifty that the only head Ianello would get tonight would be his own . . . wrapped in towels and placed on his lap.

Benny had heard rumors—fairly reliable ones—that maybe someone in this group here tonight had cooperated with the feds, maybe even worn a wire for a while. And that there was a very good chance that the capo, who had spent the last couple of weeks in court, was going to serve time. Benny had no idea if any of this was true or not. In his circle, rumors flew like sparrows at Capistrano. But if it were true, his money was on Ianello, who had more knowledge of where family money came from and went to than maybe anyone but the guys at the top.

The guys all had drinks and were sitting around a big table at the back of the restaurant, one that couldn't be seen from the street outside. Benny had set the table earlier that evening. As a chef, he didn't usually do that, but the higher-ups had instructed that there would be no wait staff or other help on this occasion. So it all fell on Benny's shoulders.

It was a pain in the ass, but he hoped—if he got through the night alive—that he'd score a few points with the bosses.

Yeah, he laughed nervously to himself.

If.

And that was going to be a big "if."

Appetizer

—

Seared foie gras
with roasted apricots & sour cherry syrup

➤ Seared Foie Gras ➤

Slice foie gras and sear until brown.
Peel and halve and pit apricots; toss with olive oil.
Roast.
In a saucepan, cook pitted cherries, sugar, red wine vinegar.
Reduce.
Puree in robot coupe.
Strain through chinois.
Cook until thick.
Toss sprouts with truffle oil.
Arrange foie gras and roasted apricots on a platter.
Pour sour cherry sauce over it.

~ First Course: Appetizer ~

Benny lowered the flame under the foie gras he was searing. This was a dish the guys probably rarely had, he thought, and it was going to blow these guys' minds. And when the roasted apricots and the sour cherry syrup were added to the dish, it would be like nothing—*nothing*—any of them ever got at home, no matter how great cooks their wives, girlfriends, or mothers were.

Benny knew the foie gras would knock the socks off the assembled gentlemen. At least, most of them. No one prepared foie gras the way Benny did, and he took extreme pride in it.

He wondered, though, if the guys would appreciate it. Some of them were likely to be extremely limited in their meal choices, never getting beyond the usual mundane antipasto and pasta dishes.

Well, he was going to change that tonight. And the guys who *really* loved fine cuisine were going to be in heaven.

At least, until the meal was finished.

As he put the finishing touches on the dishes, Benny eavesdropped on the conversations going on between the men at the occupied table and those still standing around the bar sucking down the free liquor as quickly as they could.

"You know what's the whole problem with these young guys?"

"These punks!"

"Yeah."

"Yeah what?"

"The problem. It's always 'take out.' Take out this one, take out that one."

"Yeah, but it's fast, it's easy. You gotta agree with that."

Benny had heard this particular subject discussed many times over the years. The veterans were always complaining about the new guys, the guys who had, for the most part, yet to prove themselves as loyal soldiers, or were "proven" but were trying to move up the ladder too quickly, without fully paying their dues or paying the proper respect to the right people.

"Yeah, I can agree with that."

"You go in. Then *bam!* It's in the bag. You come out in no time flat. And on to serious business. You know what I mean?"

"I hear you."

"It's not like there's always time for a sit-down."

"I'm not saying that."

"So what the hell are you saying?"

Benny shook his head, smiling to himself. Same old topic. The old guys bitching about the new guys. So what else was new?

And, actually, Benny realized that discussions weren't much different outside this restaurant, outside this family. Everywhere there were old guys squawking about the new breed, whoever they were, whatever they did. Yogi Berra or Whitey Ford spoke about how the "new" baseball heroes—pumped up on steroids and using corked bats—weren't really as good as the old boys like Mickey

Mantle or Warren Spahn. Sinatra knocked the Beatles back in the day—when they first hit American shores—saying their music was noise and wouldn't last. Old folks complained that there hadn't been any "real" comedy on television since "Uncle" Milton Berle and Sid Caesar went off the air. Even average, modern-day baby-boomer parents complain that they were better students than their own kids are because they didn't have calculators or computers to help them back when they were children.

Same old discussion, Benny thought.

Same old shit.

But Benny wondered about the wisdom of holding these discussions in such detail. If, as it had been reported in the press, the feds had incriminating tapes that implicated the capo, they probably got them from informal conversations like these one going on right now, during which someone had a wire taped to his chest.

One of the guys sitting out there in the dining room could be wearing a wire now, he thought. He wouldn't put it past someone like Palumbo. Or Ischia. Or any of them, really.

Benny stopped thinking about it. He could go down the list of all the men present here tonight and still not know. No one was going to insult any of these guys by checking them for a wire or asking too many tactless questions. He sure as hell wasn't.

But he *was*, he decided, going to watch what he said and did.

His attention turned back to the discussions in the dining room.

"I'm saying that these young guys don't know any better. The 'take-out' thing is not the only solution."

"Yeah, but it's their thing."

"Yeah."

"And as the low man on the totem pole, it's their responsibility."

"Yeah."

"And if the man upstairs doesn't mind . . ."

"Now wait a second. The man upstairs doesn't have a problem with the 'take-out' thing because he gets to do things by his own set of rules. I mean, it's not like *he* has to go hungry when things get rough."

Benny wasn't generally very interested in who was saying what to whom, but he arched his neck to see who it was who was knocking the capo. It didn't really surprise Benny when he realized it was Ischia, perhaps the most "mysterious" of the lot of them.

"Remember the time the man upstairs was fuckin' upset about Marino's closing his restaurant for that second honeymoon?"

Oh no, Benny thought, not the Marino story again.

"Yeah."

"Well, I had to do a drop-off there the next day, and lo and fuckin' behold, what do I see? Marino stretched out on a table in the back, his linen shirt the color of marinara, with little chunks of meat all around. What a mess that place was."

"The man was upset, so someone came up with a solution."

"Damn straight! Fuckin' Wall-Eyed Willy told Marino that he better make some final arrangements before he left, but the stupid shit didn't listen. He works all fuckin' night. The next thing you know Marino never makes the plane for that second honeymoon."

Benny arranged the foie gras on a platter. He had heard this tale about Marino before, too. And although he wasn't anywhere near the scene, nor was he in any way involved in it, he felt he could have told the story more quickly than whoever was doing the talking.

"What about Marino's wife?"

"She was already in Aruba, and man, was she pissed!"

"No kidding."

"What could she expect? The man was up all night making a week's worth of marinara with meat sauce for the man upstairs. Marino must've been exhausted. The son of a bitch passed out right there in the kitchen. Probably spilled a day and a half's worth of sauce all over the place when he fell."

"He finished the sauce, though."

"Of course. He wasn't stupid. The man upstairs gets what the man upstairs wants, right?"

"You got it."

Benny looked over his appetizers one last time. Sigh. Sometimes these guys were more repetitious than *Star Trek* and *I Love Lucy* reruns combined on the local network. He added a few Chinese apple pomegranate seeds to garnish where he felt they were needed to make the dishes more visually presentable.

"Marino did catch the next flight south on the following day?"

"Yeah, but that's not all he caught. He caught his wife with a spic cabana boy doing the indoor/outdoor plumbing in the honeymoon suite that Marino had already paid for."

"I guess she didn't think he was coming."

"Well, she fuckin' thought wrong. She made a *big* mistake."

"And the spic paid for it."

"The man upstairs was happy to oblige. He even sent one of the gaga girls down to keep him company."

"Hey, why not? The man knows good marinara with meat sauce is hard to find."

"Fuckin' A!"

As if on cue—the oft-repeated saga of Marino and his marinara being over—Benny entered from the kitchen, holding a crystal platter in each hand.

"Gentlemen," he announced, "start cumming!"

He placed the platters on the table, one on each end.

"Goddamn, Benny," Aspromonte said. "Those plates are so gorgeous I hate to mess 'em up."

"But you will," Benny wisecracked. "Or these other guys will beat you to it."

"Fuck that!" Aspromonte responded, moving one of the dishes closer to him and grabbing the silver serving spoon.

"Enjoy, gentlemen," Benny said, bowing slightly. "I've got to return to the studio to create my next work of art."

Then he turned and reentered the kitchen.

He knew he had a couple of minutes before he really had to do anything, so Benny grabbed his coat, searched through his pockets for his pack of Marlboro Lights and his Zippo lighter engraved with the E Street Band logo. Stepping outside the side door of the restaurant into the cold night air, Benny fished a smoke out of the pack, stuck it between his lips, and lit it.

Benny was always happy when he was cooking; he felt it was his true vocation, his *real* calling. Even after a long day of preparing meals at his restaurant he would often go home and relax by creating something in the kitchen for his wife and kids. And on those rare occasions when he took a day off from Pazzo Oeuf he liked nothing better than cooking at home while watching the Knicks or the Yankees—depending on which time of year it was—on television.

Regina, his queen (her real name was Deanne, but he called her his *regina*), *loved* his cooking and also loved the fact that *she* didn't have to cook that often. Even Benny's kids, as young as they were, ate almost everything he whipped up. He was glad they would be growing up with a real appreciation of the culinary arts, unlike many kids, whose parents thought a trip to Burger King or opening a supermarket-bought frozen dinner was giving their kids a balanced diet and exposure to a variety of foods.

Benny realized that many of the guys sitting in the dining room were like those kids. They would eat almost anything he would cook, but most of them had *no* appreciation for the artistry or workmanship that went into preparing a great meal.

He found that fact frustrating sometimes, but had learned to deal with it. Not everyone could appreciate Michelangelo's *Pietà* either, he reasoned.

He sucked in another drag of his cigarette, then let it out in a long exhale. His mind wandered, although he tried to keep focused on the meal he had to present. But his thoughts drifted anyway.

How the hell did I wind up here? he wondered. Cooking for a bunch of goombahs, one of whom was probably going to wind up tonight with two slugs in his brain.

Or it could be me, he thought.

Fuck!

Had it all come to this? Was *this* the big payoff for all his work, all the bullshit he'd been through? All he ever wanted to do was to work in the kitchen of somewhere like Commander's Palace in New Orleans. Being the head chef in a place of that caliber was his ultimate goal.

How the hell did I wind up here? he wondered.

He flipped the butt into the street and watched as the red tip sparked as it hit the pavement.

He stepped back into the kitchen. The warmth of the ovens felt good and quickly took the chill out of his bones.

He leaned against the counter, unconsciously shaking his head. No, this isn't what I had in mind when I got started, he thought. Not at all. I just wanted to be a world-class chef, that's all . . .

. . . Culinary school was a fucking waste of time.

Benny had thought about switching to a school for culinary arts when he was attending college, but from what he knew about the programs from people he had spoken to and the brochures the schools themselves had sent him at his request, it seemed like a bigger sea of shit than he was willing to sail through.

So he learned the way he wanted to: by getting the experience firsthand, by working in any restaurant that would hire him. Learning on the job was the way to go for him. And that's what he did, though it had taken some strategy, a bit of exaggeration of his background, and a few big lies to break in.

While his friends had wasted their time watching crap like *Three's Company* and *Starsky and Hutch* on television, Benny had watched cooking shows on PBS, though he never let his friends know that for fear of being ragged on endlessly. The last thing he wanted to deal with then was a bunch of assholes from the Gravesend section of Brooklyn knowing he had a "thing" for Julia Child. In his mind he really didn't care about that, because even at a young age he knew he was destined to make his career in the kitchen. But who wanted to have his balls busted all the time at school or in the pool hall or bowling alley?

Also, while his peers were struggling through books such as *Portrait of the Artist as a Young Man* and *Crime and Punishment* for their college literature courses, or wasting time on magazines like *National Lampoon* or *Rolling Stone*, Benny was reading cookbooks by Jacques Pépin and Graham Kerr, the so-called "Galloping Gourmet." He was, in fact, reading everything that he could get his hands on that had even a passing relationship with anything culinary.

But Benny wasn't *all* about cooking. There was another side to him.

He also read *Sports Illustrated* on a regular basis.

When he was younger, Benny had wanted to become a professional baseball player. Like many kids, his ultimate dream was to run out onto the infield of Yankee Stadium and hear the cheers of the fans echoing throughout the Bronx stadium. Benny was still in good shape back then and played second base on his high school baseball team. He also played hockey and football—mostly "street" hockey and touch football—but baseball was his great love.

Next to cooking, that is.

It was simply amazing the amount of information and the number of recipes Benny had absorbed simply by reading books and magazines. After a while, he felt he had a good foundation to pursue a career in the world of culinary arts.

At least, he thought so.

What he was sure of was that he had enough information and grasp of culinary lingo that he could show up at a restaurant, ask for work, and, even though he had no experience whatsoever, bullshit his way in.

Which is precisely what he did.

The day after he turned twenty Benny entered a restaurant specializing in French and northern Italian cuisine on Avenue M in the Midwood section of Brooklyn.

It was called Napoleon.

Benny knew a girl—Rita Cafone—from his high school days whose parents owned the place. He had thought that connection might help him get his foot in the door. And he was right. After speaking to the girl's mother and the head chef—who took an instant liking to Benny's attitude and enthusiasm—and tossing around some kitchen terminology and a recipe idea or two that he had copped from one of Pépin's cookbooks, he was hired. He started the next day, helping the chef and his assistants with the food preparation and its proper storage.

Benny was happy to be working in a restaurant, though shredding carrots and peeling onions was a great distance from what he really wanted to be doing: creating masterful meals. But he was willing to put in the time and pay his dues performing everyday tasks, so he worked diligently and reliably under the direction of the chef and Rita's mother.

Everything went well for a few days.

Then, one night a week later Mrs. Cafone walked into the kitchen near closing time (after the chef had gone home and left Benny to clean up) and saw her daughter kneeling in front of Benny in a corner of the kitchen. Benny hadn't seen Mrs. Cafone come in. He was much too engrossed in the lips that were wrapped around his cock.

Mrs. Cafone flew into a rage and told him in very blunt language to "get his ass" out of her restaurant. Benny was mortified, but the chef, a balding man with a mustache that stood out like Salvatore Dalí's, was absolutely shocked when he got an extremely angry call later that night from Mrs. Cafone.

Benny hurriedly pulled up his pants, threw his apron on a counter, and left the restaurant. He wanted to get the hell out of there as quickly as possible. He knew he'd get something a lot worse than fired if *Mr.* Cafone showed up.

He ran out into the street and headed toward Ocean Parkway. He didn't even know where he was headed; he just wanted to get away from Napoleon.

He just wanted to clear his head. But that wasn't easy.

He was stunned by all that had happened in the past hour. One minute he was cleaning pots and pans. The next he was talking to Rita, who had wandered into the kitchen nonchalantly.

They hadn't spoken to each other in years, and Benny was simply amazed when, after some very mild flirting back and forth between them, she had pushed him against a wall, unzipped his pants, knelt on the floor, and took him in her mouth.

Shit like this just doesn't happen, he thought.

It just doesn't.

Not in real life.

Not in a sane world.

Not to me.

But then he remembered something. Rita was a psycho. Not the Charles Manson kind of psycho. More like the drugged-up space cadet kind.

As he walked farther down Avenue M, he remembered something about Rita and one particular incident from their school days.

One night after a party, he had walked Rita home. The two of them and their classmates had just graduated from the eighth grade of Our Lady of Mercy Grammar School and Irene Cordela, who had been in their class, had a party in the basement of her parents' house. It was the usual "spin the bottle" party that adolescents have . . . or at least did in those days. After the festivities, Benny walked Rita home, hoping that maybe he'd get a kiss—maybe even a little tongue interplay—from her.

Outside her door, in the shadow of a drab green canopy that hung out over the driveway next to her house, Rita held Benny's face with both hands while she drove her tongue into his mouth so hard that their teeth clacked when their mouths met. Benny just stood there enjoying it. Her tongue wiggled in his mouth for several minutes, and Benny felt a stirring in his pants. And since Rita wasn't letting up, Benny took it as a sign that cupping her thirteen-year-old breast outside her sweater might be alright with her. So that's what he did.

Then suddenly Rita stopped cold, no more touching, no more tongue.

No more words.

She turned away from Benny, gave him an exasperated look, opened her door, and went inside.

Benny just stood there, mortified and confused. What the hell just happened? he wondered.

Had he gone too far, not far enough?

Was she insulted, frightened off?

Who the fuck knew what a woman thought?

Benny didn't move for a while, wondering if Rita would come back outside. She never did.

So he left a few minutes later, walked home, and after that night never gave the incident another thought.

Until that night in Napoleon. He realized that he and Rita had never really spoken again until that night.

And then, after a few words back and forth, she blows me, he thought. Was this whole thing her way of making up for that night long ago? Or was she still pissed off about it and did all this just to get him fired? He didn't know; he didn't want to know.

What he *did* know was that she was one crazy broad! And he hoped he wouldn't run into her for another eight years or so.

So his first job in a restaurant was short-lived. But at least he knew he had the ability to get hired, even if it meant bullshitting a little. And now, at least, he did have *some* experience.

Benny recalled his parents' attitude toward his choice of career when he first told them he wanted to be a chef.

They didn't quite understand it, especially his father, who was a hardworking man who had had a civil service position most of his life. But neither of his parents ever did anything to actively discourage him, although his father would occasionally drop hints that he should go to college and study so he could pursue a "real" career.

And then there were his father's insinuations about Benny's uncle Tony, who had his own restaurant in Bensonhurst. Benny's dad would inevitably shake his head in disappointment at the very mention of Tony, as if he were a lost sheep. This always came as a surprise to Benny, because he was well aware that Uncle Tony had the best car and the biggest house out of all the members of the Lacoco family. When his dad would ask, "You don't want to wind up like your uncle Tony, do you?" Benny would wonder why not.

After the week at Napoleon, Benny managed to parlay that week's worth of experience into a very detailed verbal résumé, which he threw at any restaurant manager who would give him the time of day. Many wanted a written résumé; others wanted a recommendation from someone at Napoleon; more simply told him to get out.

But the manager of Bayou, a fancy new eatery on the west side of Manhattan specializing in Cajun cuisine, decided he liked young Benny's nerve and bravado and hired him on the spot, without asking for any references whatsoever. Benny had told the manager, who appeared to be high on something or other, that he could do whatever the manager wanted in the kitchen: food prep, sauces, gumbos, anything, everything. And Mr. D'Hubert, with his slicked back hair drawn into a ponytail and his ever glossy eyes, started Benny that very weekend.

Benny, however, lasted on the job only until the following Saturday night. It was then that the head chef of Bayou, meat cleaver in hand, threatened to cut Benny's balls off and keep them in a glass jar in the kitchen if he ever set foot in his kitchen again—as a warning to the rest of his staff. When D'Hubert answered the panicky call of one of the chef's assistants and entered the kitchen, he found the chef wielding the cleaver over his head and screaming like a lunatic . . . and Benny only a few feet away from him with a huge, shiny silver knife in his hand.

An hour later Benny was sitting on the B train to Brooklyn with $109 in his pocket—at least he was paid for his two and a half days' work—thinking that maybe he shouldn't have exaggerated his kitchen abilities quite so much. He hadn't been able to live up to the claims he had made to D'Hubert. And D'Hubert's chef caught on to that fact early on.

But an even bigger mistake was sampling a small piece of the chef's blackened catfish without asking. And then wrinkling his nose because it was *way* too spicy, so much so that the taste of the fish was all but gone. Then Benny removed the mouthful of catfish, one of the chef's masterpieces, from his mouth with a napkin and dropped the morsel into a trash can.

All within sight of the chef!

No, not a good idea, Benny thought, as the train rolled into Pacific Street.

Things went this way for quite some time. Benny managed to get on-the-job training in several other restaurants in Brooklyn and downtown Manhattan. He would do whatever they wanted him to, everything from food buying to food preparation to waiting tables. And he continued his self-education by borrowing all of the newly published cookbooks from the Brooklyn Public Library and reading them from cover to cover. When he discovered a particularly great book, he would buy it from Brentano's or one of the bookstores in the Kings Plaza mall.

On weekends, when Benny would go drinking with his friends—most of the time in any of several bars in Bay Ridge, where it seemed to be much easier to pick up girls, perhaps because of all the Catholic schools in the neighborhood—he would tell them stories of some of the shit that went down in some of the places he had worked or was currently working in. And Benny had some disgusting tales to tell about the less than healthy conditions of some of the eateries.

But no story was ever gross enough for his friends. They wanted to know if anyone ever fucked on the counters in the kitchen.

Benny would laugh along with them, but even his friends—many of whom were from "connected" families—knew that Benny was serious about the culinary arts and the food business. One of these friends, Leo Ranallo, talked to his father, who "oversaw" a few restaurants in Brooklyn, and told him about Benny. Two days later, on a Monday, by which time Benny and Leo had mostly slept off and worked off their Saturday night bender, Benny received a call from Leo. Leo's dad had a job for Benny if he wanted it. He would be trained as an assistant chef in Franzo's, in Dyker Heights.

Benny was surprised. But he was even more amused and bewildered.

Benny had worked at Franzo's before, from the time he was twelve years old until he was about fourteen. He would sweep the place then. He would wash dishes. He would do pretty much whatever the manager wanted him to do.

That's because the manager was his uncle Tony. As far as Benny knew, he still was. But evidently Leo's dad had a lot of input in decisions regarding Franzo's.

This phone call from Leo linked forever Benny's past and his future.

Benny started working at his uncle Tony's the very next week.

He hadn't really had any extended contact with his uncle over the previous few years, except on holidays, when the families would get together at Tony's house on Seventy-first Street and Tenth Avenue and feast on turkey, lasagna, and brasciole for hours. And, of course, after Christmas dinner, the whole family— in fact, the whole neighborhood—would stand across the street from Tony's house and marvel at the garish Christmas display that adorned his uncle's house, his lawn, and, seemingly every inch of his property. Even as a young boy Benny realized that his uncle probably had more reindeer on his lawn and roof than Santa had at the North Pole.

When Benny started that first Tuesday evening—Franzo's was closed on Mondays, like many restaurants and practically every Italian barber shop in Brooklyn—he noticed how old his uncle looked. He couldn't have been more than fifty-one or fifty-two, but the lines in his face, the wrinkles on his forehead, and the bags under his eyes made him look well over sixty.

His face seemed to have a perpetual frown on it, as if he were deeply concerned about something all the time. And the guy could curse. Benny and his friends were never shy when it came to "bad" language—cursing being an art form among the young in Brooklyn—but Benny *never* heard *anything* like the flow of filth that emanated from his uncle's mouth, especially when his uncle was alone and thought no one could hear him.

Often, Tony would be in the back room going over the books or checking receipts or counting the cash, and Benny, who was letting the diavolo sauce simmer, would hear the verbal onslaught: fucking this, cocksucker that, motherfucking goddamn sonof-abitch bastard ass-licking cunt fucker. . . . Sometimes this stream would be in English exclusively, but more often than not it was a blend of Italian and English and God knew what else.

Of course, when Tony was around his customers, his friends, and his family, there was none of this. He appeared to not have a care in the world.

Benny wondered if Uncle Tony was schizophrenic. But he suspected there was something Uncle Tony was hiding from everyone, something to do with several shady, tough-looking guys who would come into the restaurant every so often to eat. They always came late, just before the place was about to close. Uncle Tony would always serve these guys himself and tell Benny to stay in the kitchen and "get tomorrow's menu ready."

One night Benny forgot to stay in the back and wandered into the dining room, and the two guys and his uncle looked at him. Uncle Tony was annoyed, but one of the other two guys smiled.

"Come here, kid," one guy said.

Benny walked up to the table.

"Can I get you something?" he asked nervously.

"No thanks, kid," the man answered. "I was just wonderin'. How old are you?"

"Twenty."

"Get the hell outta here!" the man laughed. "I bet you're only about seventeen."

"No, I'm twenty," Benny corrected.

"Yeah? What's your favorite football team?"

"The Giants."

"Of course," he laughed. "The home team. You ever 'play'?"

Uncle Tony swiveled in his seat. "C'mon, Ricky, don't . . ."

The man named Ricky held up his hand. Uncle Tony immediately stopped protesting.

"I'm just askin' the kid a question. Right, kid?"

"Yeah," Benny said.

"So, you ever play?"

Benny knew he was talking about gambling.

"I've been in football pools."

"I ain't talkin' about no pools. You know what I'm askin', don't you?"

"You mean bet through a bookie?"

Ricky nodded, smiling a big grin. "You could say that."

"Not really," Benny answered honestly. "But some of my friends have."

"You know your football? You could make a lot of money if you do."

"I guess."

Uncle Tony started to say, "Or you could lose . . ." But, once again, Ricky held up his hand and cut him off.

"Want to bet on this week's games?"

Benny just stood still, not saying a word.

Ricky looked at him hard. "You shy, kid, or what? I'll tell you what. You take this. I have a friend who can take care of it for you." Then he handed Benny a card with a telephone number on it. "You ever want to make a bet, you call that number."

"Thanks," Benny said.

"Now get lost," Ricky said. "Your uncle and us have important business to attend to."

Benny retreated to the kitchen and stared at the number on the card. Then he shoved the card in the right pocket of the black dress pants he had to wear at the restaurant.

A few minutes later Uncle Tony came into the kitchen. He looked like he had been to hell and back.

"Throw that card away, Benny," he said.

"I already did," Benny lied.

Uncle Tony forced a smile and went into the back room.

Benny listened for the stream of curses, but this night there weren't any. So, after a few minutes, Benny asked his uncle if he could leave.

"Good night," he heard through the door. He also heard the clinking of a bottle on the rim of a glass.

During the course of the next few days, the pieces of the puzzle that was his uncle's situation began to fit together. Pretty obviously, these guys were into Uncle Tony for some money, probably a great deal. That would also explain Benny's father's attitude toward him, since his father wasn't a player in that league at all. Sure, he might play the occasional numbers or put a few bucks in a World Series pool at work, or trek over to Belmont Park to play the horses every once in a while, but that was the extent of it. His dad's motto—which Benny had heard over and over again since he was a young kid—was "neither a lender nor a borrower be."

Benny, however, chose to ignore the motto.

Before the end of the week he called the phone number the man named Ricky had given him. Benny had carefully checked the point spread on the upcoming pro football games and bet on several of those scheduled for the coming Sunday. He bet twenty-dollar straight bets on five different games, and when he hung up the phone, he took a deep breath.

Why was he doing this? To get easy money? To maybe help his uncle Tony out? He wasn't sure, and deep inside his brain he knew he should have had more sense. But what the hell, he thought, it was only a hundred bucks.

On Sunday night, after the games were over, he knew he had picked winners, but wasn't exactly sure of how much cash he had won. He thought about taking some of the money and giving it to his uncle, but he knew that if he did, Uncle Tony might get on his case for gambling at all.

Ricky said he would take care of it for him. The bookie was a friend of his, and if Benny came up short on a week, Ricky could let him know and even offer to cover for him for a slight fee.

So he kept quiet.

And he continued betting. And picking up betting tips and strategies from some of his friends and one of the older waiters at Franzo's.

The next week he played a two-team teaser. He came out ahead. The week after that he tried betting the over/under on a few games. The Giants, *his* team as he liked to think of them, and the Vikings didn't let him down.

He felt like he was on a winning streak.

This continued for a while. Benny would just put his winnings back into the next week's games. A real green paper dollar never crossed his palm. But he knew he was way in the black and felt like he had some magic charm or some psychic sense that enabled him to score big.

A few weeks later he figured he might have enough to actually help his uncle out a little, since there were no signs that Uncle Tony had bettered his own situation.

In fact, the opposite was true.

Benny had seen Ricky in the restaurant late one night just before closing time, and he heard Ricky screaming at his uncle, pounding his fist so hard on one of the tables that all the dishes and glasses bounced off the tabletop from the impact, crashed to the floor, and broke into pieces.

Benny wanted to offer Ricky some of his winnings to help his uncle out, but he didn't. He was scared. And he thought he'd wait a couple more weeks; hopefully, by then Benny's wad of winnings would be more substantial.

So Benny tried to ignore the whole situation for a while, confident that in a couple of weeks he'd have enough to lessen some of his uncle's debt. Surely, Uncle Tony wouldn't break his balls for gambling if he helped bail him out.

And Benny thought about his own future, too. He would stop rolling over his winnings. Instead, he would collect and start investing in his own future. In his own career. In his own *restaurant*! Imagine, he thought.

Then the weekend came and went. The Sunday games and Monday night football were over.

Unlike most Monday nights around midnight, Benny wasn't relaxed, thinking about Howard Cosell's verbal jibes or Frank

Gifford's color commentary on the *Monday Night Football* broadcast. This time he had other things to think about.

Like how not a single one of his football picks had come out right this weekend.

Like how he had blown more cash than he had ever had before.

Like how he wondered if he even had enough money to pay what Ricky had called vig. Two points instead of the usual two and a half.

Like how this must be a fluke, just a momentary bad turn of the wheel of fortune.

Like how he'd established a trust with the people at the phone number Ricky had given him . . . and with Ricky.

And like how he would go ahead and bet this week, even though he didn't have shit to bet with. He was confident it would all turn around again the next week, and the week after that.

The only thing that changed, though, was Benny's roster of friends.

One night, as Benny was smoking a cigarette outside Franzo's, he was approached by a man who introduced himself simply as Napoli. He calmly told Benny that Ricky wanted to know what Benny planned to do. Benny asked what he meant.

Napoli said that Benny owed Ricky and his friend. Benny's jaw dropped when he heard the amount and the Marlboro dropped from his lips to the sidewalk.

It couldn't be, Benny thought. In reality, he hadn't been keeping a real tally of his winnings and losses. Ricky's people *had*, that was clear. How the hell was he going to come up with that kind of money?

Napoli provided a simple answer. Ricky'd advance him more than enough money to cover his debt just this once. And the next time Benny won, he could pay Napoli back. . . . but no knock-down payments. All paid at once or the interest grew.

Nervous but partially relieved, Benny accepted the offer, even after he heard the exorbitant rate of interest on the loan. He knew the guy was a shylock, but he was still confident that his earlier winnings were not simply a case of beginner's luck.

The deal was all very friendly.

Very civilized.

He'd be even and ahead in no time.

It wasn't until the next week that Benny truly realized he had been very stupid.

After getting a phone call at the restaurant, Uncle Tony walked up to Benny in the kitchen. Benny was wrapping food and putting it all away, some in the refrigerator, some in the freezer.

"Benny, do me a favor," Uncle Tony said. "I'm feeling like shit tonight. Would you mind locking up for me?"

"No," Benny answered. "I can lock up. And you don't look too good, Uncle Tony. Everything okay?"

"Just feel like shit, that's all. Got a big freaking headache. Must have drunk too much wine."

"I'll finish wrapping, then lock up. Unless there's anything else you need me to do."

"No, that'll be fine. I already told the staff to go home."

Benny put a couple of dozen plum tomatoes in a paper bag and shoved the bag onto a crowded shelf. "Okay. I got the spare key."

Uncle Tony grabbed his overcoat and walked out the side door. "See you tomorrow, kid."

"Yeah, see ya."

Benny looked around the kitchen, then stepped out into the dining area. Everything seemed okay, so he reached for his coat, put it on, and stepped outside. He locked the door, then tugged at the doorknob to make sure it had locked properly. He walked to the front entrance and tried the door there too.

All secure.

The streets were quiet. There didn't seem to be anyone around, except for a guy who was sitting in the driver's seat in a Lincoln Town Car across the avenue. The car was running, and even from across the street Benny could hear the guy had his stereo blasting. He could even make out the song. It was "Hold On Loosely" by .38 Special.

Benny turned to head home and practically walked into a man who braced himself against their colliding bodies by holding his forearms out in front of him.

Momentarily shocked, Benny looked into Ricky's smiling eyes.

"Hey, kid! How ya doin'?" he asked.

"Uh . . . okay, I guess," Benny managed to answer.

"Yeah, that's good," Ricky said, grabbing Benny's arm the way a boy holds an old lady's arm when he's helping her across the street. "But we got to talk."

Then he helped Benny across the street.

"Get in the car."

Benny knew better than to resist. While Ricky opened the rear door for him, Benny realized that the driver was the man—he still didn't know his name—who always accompanied Ricky. Benny slid over and sank into the cushiony rear seat. Something inside him sank too. It might have been his stomach.

Ricky sat next to him, and without a word being spoken the driver made a U-turn and then turned onto Eighty-sixth Street. In total silence the car headed up a couple of blocks, then turned into the small parking lot outside the golf course.

When the driver turned the engine off, Benny's heart practically jumped into his throat. Ricky threw an arm around him, pulled him close, and said, "Now here's the deal, kid . . ."

Ricky went on about the ever growing sum of money that Benny owed and how he was going to cut Benny a break because he was just a kid and maybe didn't understand how this shit all worked but debts got to be paid or there's consequences and how he should ask his uncle Tony about that and nobody really wants to hurt anybody but everybody's got to answer to somebody else in this world and then there's Napoli, . . . and . . . and . . .

All Ricky's words eventually blurred in his mind, but somehow Benny heard and understood every one of them. Except maybe during the moment when Ricky pulled a revolver out of his pocket and used it as a tool to emphasize his points.

Then Ricky asked Benny if he understood.

Benny said, "Yes . . . sir."

Ricky smiled and tapped his friend, the driver, on the shoulder. "Did I tell you or what? He's a good kid. Respectful and all that. 'Sir'! I like that."

The driver turned and looked Benny square in the eyes. "So then you don't want me to break his kneecap like you said before?" he asked.

Benny closed his eyes. He thought his heart was going to burst.

Ricky laughed. "Nah. I was just in a fucked-up mood before."

Then the car pulled out of the parking lot back onto Eighty-sixth Street. A moment later Benny was dropped off where he had been picked up.

"See you, kid," Ricky said. "Remember what I said. You don't got much time. And that debt's growing, and no knockdowns. See you soon." Ricky pointed the gun playfully at Benny and laughed.

The Town Car sped off and made the first left turn. Benny didn't know whether to run, try to get some help, or just cry.

He did none of those things. He just went home and tried to sleep. But he couldn't. His mind was racing. His blood was pounding its way through his veins. And he was sweating heavily.

This sucks, he thought. This *really* sucks. What the fuck am I gonna do? What the *fuck* am I gonna do?

He sat up in his bed and took a deep breath. First thing, I gotta calm down. Can't think straight all fucked up like this. Gotta calm down.

He turned his television on but kept the sound low so as not to wake up his parents. He flipped around the dial until he saw that an episode of *The Honeymooners* was on. It was one that he had seen a couple of dozen times. He had seen them *all* a couple of dozen times. It was the "Chef of the Future" episode, one of many in which Ralph Kramden came up with a get-rich-quick scheme that went bad.

Benny knew the message of this episode—like most of the others—was "be happy with what you have" and "get-rich-quick schemes don't work." But that was exactly what Benny needed. He needed cash and he needed it fast. He needed it *yesterday* if possible.

Betting on sports had stopped working out. He had to come up with something that he was more familiar with. Something he knew well. Something that couldn't fail. Something that would bring him a lot of money fast, something that would deliver . . .

Deliver. Deliver. Delivery.

Then it occurred to him. He knew where he might be able to make a go of it.

Food delivery service.

No.

Better yet, *gourmet* food delivery service.

He could prepare the food himself. He could deliver it himself. It *could* work. It had to work.

Gourmet Express took a few weeks to catch on, and Benny sweated out every single second of those weeks. But he was determined to make it work, and his staunch determination—and his fear—got it going.

Benny wrote up a sample menu of meals he knew he could cook up quickly using supplies and food from his uncle's restaurant. Since one of the latest responsibilities his uncle had given him was ordering the food for Franzo's, it wouldn't be that difficult for Benny to order more chicken, shrimp, and beef than the restaurant really needed.

Furthermore, since Uncle Tony had taken to drinking a lot more and paying less attention to details at the restaurant, Benny figured he could actually cook the meals after closing time and store some of them in the restaurant's freezer. And when he went home after the place closed, he could prepare some of the food in his mother's kitchen, sometimes at one or two o'clock in the morning. (He probably could have stayed at Franzo's after closing time; after all, his uncle had him closing up shop on a regular basis now, but Benny was afraid that Ricky might show up at the restaurant, and he didn't want that to happen. Ricky was the last person he wanted to see under *any* circumstances.)

Benny's plans all worked out. He used Franzo's as his base, but the operation was spreading. After distributing his flyer to a few dozen homes and nearby small businesses—a flyer that he designed and typed himself—he had a number of customers in just a few days.

Benny knew at that point that he had to get *some* help in this venture. The phone number he used for Gourmet Express was his home phone. He asked his mom to take the orders, telling her he was starting his own business. She was glad to do it and was very proud of her son's creativity and business acumen. Of course, Benny never told her anything about his gambling debts.

Benny also got a friend involved. Joey Arso was a reliable guy and one of the few people in the neighborhood that he trusted completely. Joey's father had been out of work as long as Benny had known him, and Joey was always picking up odd jobs here and there to make a few extra bucks because his part-time job at Sounds Unlimited, the record store, didn't pay shit.

Joey was happy to become Benny's deliveryman.

They worked out a schedule where Joey would call Benny at home or at Franzo's every hour to see if he was needed to make a delivery. On occasion, Benny would make the delivery himself, but more often than not, he was at the restaurant or preparing the food in his mom's kitchen.

Benny eventually wrote up a revised menu and lowballed the prices he charged. He could afford to do that since most of the food was coming gratis via his uncle. Then he covered a small area of Bensonhurst that he knew would be convenient to him, to Joey, and to Franzo's. A folded one-page black-and-white flyer was stuffed into home mailboxes from Twelfth to Eighteenth avenues, from Bath Avenue to Seventy-fifth Street.

After a couple of days, many more calls started coming in. For the first week after he had distributed the revised flyer, Gourmet Express averaged twelve to fourteen calls a day. Benny would prepare the food; Joey would deliver it; and the two would split the money, Benny getting two-thirds and Joey getting the remaining third and keeping whatever tip was involved.

Benny was beginning to make some money. It wasn't a hell of a lot, but it was something. Benny knew that with every day that passed, the interest on his "loan" was growing. And the couple of hundred dollars a week that he was making wouldn't make a goddamn dent in that debt.

The next few weeks changed all that. The combination of more flyers being distributed and the word-of-mouth conveyed by a happy customer or two caused a big boost in business. After one particularly hectic day, Benny realized he'd have to get more help to keep up with the orders. His mom, beaming with pride at her son's impending success, agreed to help prepare some of the meals at home for delivery. Her job was mostly just to cook the already prepared food according to Benny's meticulously detailed instructions. Joey recruited a couple more friends to help with the deliveries. These drivers were paid a couple of bucks per delivery and got to keep any tips.

Then, one night, Benny locked his bedroom door, removed a cigar box from his dresser at home, and opened it. In it was all the money—all the profits—from the Gourmet Express's first few weeks of business. Benny removed his wallet from his pocket and added the cash he had gotten from his uncle for working at Franzo's.

Thirty-three hundred dollars.

Benny smiled. He'd never had that much cash in front of him in his life.

Then he tried to figure out what he owed Ricky. He juggled some numbers with a pencil on a piece of paper, but it was useless. Math was never his best subject in school, and the whole loanshark system was fucking impossible for him to comprehend.

He sat back in his chair, just a little relieved. He couldn't owe *that* much more than five, maybe five and a half grand. Having at least most of the money might save him from a pair of broken legs . . . or whatever these wise guys did to people who owed them money. And he had heard some wicked stories about that through the grapevine.

Well, fuck that.

Benny wasn't about to let that happen to him.

No way.

He thought about the prospect of Gourmet Express *really* taking off. If all went well, he might one day have enough to live out one of his dreams: to open his own restaurant. Not just squaring himself with the sharks. Not just creating world-class meals for other restaurant owners. Having his *own* place was his goal, having his name known far and wide. Having famous people seek out his place—hell, *places*, why think small?—and dining on his masterpieces.

That's what Benny wanted.

That was his aim.

But he'd have to pay off his debt first. And if he could somehow win the favor of certain influential people who were now down on him, he might stand an even better chance.

Meanwhile, he had more than enough to think about. Besides Ricky and Napoli and their associates, Benny had to pray that his uncle didn't catch on to his side business.

Benny wasn't much good at praying, though. He did, however, put the St. Christopher medal his aunt Rosalie had given him around his neck.

Maybe it would help.

He figured it wouldn't hurt.

Soup

Crawfish bisque

Escarole with white beans & prosciutto

Crawfish Bisque

*In a big pot, combine crawfish, water, white wine, carrots, celery, onions,
bay leaf, thyme, peppercorns, tomato paste, parsley stems.
Cook until flavor is abstracted.
Strain.
Put liquid back on heat.
Add cream and thicken.
Add brandy.
Add strained crawfish meat.
Add salt and pepper to taste.*

Escarole with White Beans & Prosciutto

*Finely slice the celery.
Mince the garlic.
Finely chop the head of escarole.
Dice the onions.
Sauté the garlic in oil until brown.
Add celery and onions; cook until soft.
Add prosciutto; cook for about another minute.
Remove from pan.
Add chicken stock and water to soup pot.
Add sauté mix.
Add white beans and escarole.
Simmer for twenty minutes.
Season with salt and pepper to taste.*

— Second Course: Soup —

Benny checked the soup he had had simmering since he brought out the foie gras. He stirred it gently, bringing some of the white beans to the surface to visually check on their tenderness. He took a spoonful of the liquid, sipped it, and leaned back satisfied. There was nothing as delicious as crawfish bisque when it was prepared right. And Benny had learned how to prepare it from the best. He had picked up some tips personally from one of the chefs in the Commander's Palace in New Orleans.

The talk in the dining area among the guys had died down a little. Most of them were still stuffing their faces with the remaining foie gras that Benny had prepared.

His friend Anthony Abbazio was telling the assembled gentlemen how he had managed to get his new Audi from a police auction, after he himself had arranged for it to be "misplaced," then confiscated by the cops. Benny couldn't hear the entire explanation, but he did pick up bits of it, pieces that involved phony identities and payoffs to several middle-level police officials.

Abbazio's "thing" was "moving" cars. Sometimes they moved

directly from ships bringing them to Newark or elsewhere to one of Double A's "lots," garages of friends who could store the vehicles until they could be further moved. Sometimes cars of the more domestic variety were lost somewhere along the delivery route after they left the factory.

Double A was a wizard with autos, though he never really told anybody how he managed to pull off his operations. Benny knew that someone up at the top must have known, but no one else seemed to. Abbazio had always been a good friend of Benny's, but even Benny knew very few details about Double A's business dealings. He didn't really want to know too much. It was better that way. For that reason, Benny had never let Double A in on much of his business either.

As Abbazio was continuing his tale to the amusement of most of the guys, the narrative was interrupted by Dominick Aspromonte's cell phone ringing. Actually, it wasn't a ring. It was a few electronic-sounding strains of "O Sole Mio" that emanated from his Nokia flip phone.

Aspromonte flipped it open, checked the number, and said, " 'Scuse me, I gotta take this call."

He got up from the table and stepped over to the bar, which he leaned on, facing away from the men at the dining table.

"Yeah, what's up?" he said into the receiver. "I'm at a meeting."

The guys at the table tried to give Aspromonte some privacy by finishing up the appetizer and the remains of the antipasto. But Aspromonte could have gone outside. Or he could have talked in a lower tone of voice. Or he could have not stood where all the guys could see his face in the mirror behind the bar.

"I told you," Aspromonte continued. "I told you I'd be over later if I could."

He listened in silence for a moment, then said, "For Christ's sake, I just gave you a grand and a half."

Then he listened again.

"Yeah, yeah," he said a bit more calmly. "Yeah, you're worth it. But holy shit, you're draining me dry!"

There must have been some reply that he welcomed on the other end of the line because he answered, "I know you'll drain me later, baby." Then he laughed.

"Alright," he continued. "Right. Right. I gotta go now. See you later."

Aspromonte flipped the phone shut, then looked up at the mirror behind the bar. He saw the reflections of all the guys at the table. They were all staring at him, and they all had shit-eating grins on their faces.

"Holy fuck, man!" he exclaimed, turning around to them and shoving his phone into his jacket pocket. "Can't a guy get a little privacy?"

Michael Ischia ignored the question. Instead, he asked his own. "I just want to know one thing. Is she worth it?"

The guys grinned.

Aspromonte headed back to the table. "Yeah, she is. I guess." He pulled out his chair and lowered himself into it. "I mean, she's like a fuckin' pelican. I never seen a chick get so much cock in her mouth."

"In your case that ain't that much," Aspromonte heard someone say.

When "Aspirin" realized it was Palumbo who had made the comment, and he was enjoying his own witticism, Aspromonte shot back, "It's enough that it choked your sister last week, jerk-off."

As usual, Pally could dole out the insults, but he couldn't handle any directed his way.

"Hey, fuck you, Assholemonte!"

Aspromonte shot up out of his chair—as did Pally—but the rest of the guys held the two apart.

Sapienza just sat calmly in his seat and looked around at the rest of the guys. "For Christ's sake, everybody cool down. We're here to eat, not get into a fuckin' war."

Anthony Abbazio concurred, saying, "He's right. Let's make the best of things. This ain't a night to be at each other's throats."

Since he already had his hands on Aspromonte's shoulders, Double A gently steered Aspromonte back down into his chair. "Take it easy, man," he said, patting Aspromonte on the back.

Just then, Benny emerged from the kitchen, circled the table, and collected the dishes the guys had already used.

"There's not a speck of food on any of these dishes," Benny observed. "I take it you gentlemen enjoyed the first course. Did you enjoy the foie gras?"

"Out of this world," Abbazio praised. "As usual."

Benny bowed in gratitude. "Thank you. I'll bring the next course then."

Palumbo cracked, "Yeah, foie gras is French for glorified liverwurst."

Benny ignored the remark.

He reentered the kitchen and reemerged with a tray with soup dishes on it. He again circled the table, placing the steaming dishes in front of his guests.

Di Pietro leaned over and sniffed at the steam emerging from his dish. "Goddamn, Benny, this smells good. What is it? Lobster bisque?"

"Close, but no cigar," Benny answered. "It's crawfish. And I guarantee you," Benny responded, "its taste will be even better than its aroma. *Mangia!* Oh, and if anyone happens to be allergic, there is also a lovely escarole with white beans. May it bring you happiness as well . . ." Benny looked at each of the men individually for a second. ". . . and, of course, peace."

Then he returned to the sanctity and the solitude of his kitchen.

Benny recalled that he had just added two of his own recipes for soups—minestrone and lentil with sausage—to his newly expanded flyer for Gourmet Express when an unexpected visitor showed up at Franzo's one afternoon.

Tonino Greco was Benny's uncle's accountant. He entered the restaurant about 3:30 in the afternoon, just after the lunch crowd had left and before even those diners who would take advantage of Franzo's early-bird specials—mostly senior citizens—would arrive for dinner.

Benny was in the kitchen, on his knees, trying to make room on the bottom shelf of the huge refrigerator for a delivery of shrimp that had just come in. Unlike the usual order, this one had twice the amount of shrimp the restaurant usually received. Benny needed that extra shrimp for his own side business.

Uncle Tony and his visitor stepped into the back office, but as they passed Benny, his uncle introduced him to Greco. Benny stood up and shook the man's hand.

"You're Tony's nephew, huh?" he said. "He keeps you busy, I see."

"Yeah," Benny replied. "It's been pretty busy lately."

Greco stared at him, seeming to search for something in his eyes. "I bet it has," he responded. "I bet it has."

Then the two men went into the back office.

Benny finished shoving the shrimp into the refrigerator. Then he washed his hands, dried them, and stepped outside the side door to have a cigarette.

The small window to Uncle Tony's office was open just a crack, but it was open just enough for Benny to make out some of their conversation. Most of the discussion concerned numbers that made little sense to Benny. But as the discussion progressed, he could hear the two men's voices getting more emphatic and considerably louder.

When he heard his uncle clearly say, "Bullshit!" he knew for sure there was going to be trouble. Benny stepped a few feet away from the window. He didn't want either of the men to know he'd been eavesdropping if they saw him outside.

Greco and Uncle Tony stepped into the kitchen and the storage areas. Benny could see them through the side doorway, since he had left the door open. Uncle Tony opened various cabinets, the refrigerator, and the freezer while Greco peered inside, occasionally writing something down, frequently shaking his head.

They were clearly in disagreement about something, and it wasn't about any gambling money that Uncle Tony might have owed. No, this had to do with the restaurant, the business.

Then, suddenly, their voices got louder.

"What the hell are you talking about?" Uncle Tony said.

"This," Greco answered emphatically. "This is what I'm talking about."

He had taken something out of the freezer and was pointing it out to Tony.

"What the fuck is this?" he asked.

"It's shrimp," Uncle Tony replied. "It says 'Ocean Seafood Supplies' right there on the box."

"Yeah, you're right, it does say that," Greco said. "But that's not all it says. It says right here: 'Crawfish.'"

Uncle Tony took the box from the accountant and inspected the smaller print. Then he opened the box and indeed saw crawfish inside.

"So the dumb bastards sent me the wrong thing. It happens sometimes, you know."

"So why's it in the freezer?" Greco asked. "Why wasn't it turned back when the delivery came? Don't you check the shit you get?"

"Of course I do," Tony answered. "Benny's been ordering and storing the stuff for the past couple of weeks. The kid probably didn't even notice it."

Outside, Benny's throat tightened. Oh shit, he muttered to himself.

Greco pulled out another box. "This is fucking crawfish too." Then he poked around deeper into the refrigerator. "And look at all this shrimp. You sell that much shrimp?"

Uncle Tony looked where Greco pointed. After a minute, he said, "Well, it *does* seem like an awful lot. More than we usually order at one time."

"Yeah, a hell of a lot more."

Disgusted and angry, Uncle Tony finally said, "Hey, what's your problem, Greco? You implying something?"

"No, I'm implying nothing," he shot back. "I'm telling you directly that something's going on here that ain't straight. Extra food orders. Crawfish and shit like that that, ain't even on your menu and never has been. Things don't jive here. Things don't jive at all."

"Ah, you're making a big deal outta nothing."

"Really?" Greco replied in an assured, snotty tone. "Look at my figures." He opened his book and pointed. "Here's the average of your previous monthly food orders."

"Yeah, okay."

"Here's your outlay for the past month. It's almost double the old number."

Exasperated, Tony let out a deep breath. "Well, okay, something's off. I'll speak to my nephew Benny about it. He just doesn't have the hang of it yet."

"No," Greco said, "*I'll* talk to him."

He saw Benny moping around outside.

"Hey, you," he called to him. "Kid! Come here."

Benny nervously walked up to him. "Yes, sir?"

"Don't 'sir' me. You're either pulling some shit here or you're a fuckin' incompetent. Either way, you're fired."

Benny didn't answer. He didn't have time to.

"You're not firing anyone," Uncle Tony said angrily. "Who the fuck are you to fire anyone here? This is my place. I hire. I fire. Not you."

"Is that right?" Greco asked. "Well, *I* keep this place running. You'd drive it into the ground all on your own."

Uncle Tony's face grew beet red. "Really? Well, we'll see about that. Right now you can get the fuck out of my place. *You're* fired, Greco. There's other accountants around. Who the fuck do you think you are?"

"You just fired *me*?" Greco demanded to know.

"Yeah, now get out."

The accountant smiled smugly, adjusted the glasses on his nose, shut his book, shoved it into his briefcase, and left by the side door without saying another word to Uncle Tony.

But as he passed Benny, he again looked deep into his eyes. Then he smiled wickedly at him. That smile, Benny could tell, was a knowing smile. One that said Benny was very likely in deep shit.

Uncle Tony went back into his office and closed the door behind him, not saying a word to Benny.

Angelo, one of the wait staff, emerged from the side door.

"What happened?" he asked Benny.

"I don't know," Benny said in reply. "I'm not sure."

The waiter, well into his forties and a longtime employee of Tony's, shook his head and added, "I hate that Greco guy. He doesn't do anything but give your uncle grief. He's a fucking *gavone* who thinks he's hot shit."

"Yeah," Benny concurred, not really knowing what to say. This had been his first meeting with Greco. But something inside told him it wasn't going to be his last.

Then Benny thought about the fact that although Angelo might be right in that Greco caused Uncle Tony nothing but grief, it wasn't just Greco this time. It was also Benny himself.

He felt he should have known that sooner or later someone would notice something.

Crawfish! he thought. What the fuck was I thinking? Why didn't I just stick to the usual Italian fare? I might have gotten away with it then. But after reading that book he had borrowed on New Orleans recipes, he just couldn't resist the temptation to expand Gourmet Express's menu. So he added a few soups and crawfish gumbo to the revised flyer that he and Joey Arso had distributed to the neighborhood.

He smacked himself on the forehead. Couldn't have stuck to shrimp, which I might have gotten away with! No, I had to make it crawfish!

Uncle Tony emerged from his office and stepped outside. He looked Benny square in the eyes.

"This is not a time for bullshitting, Benny," he said emotionlessly. "Did you fuck up on those orders . . . or did you just fuck up?"

Benny stared back blankly.

"You know what I'm talking about. Was this all a mistake or are you into something I don't know about but should?"

"Jesus, Uncle Tony, I don't know what to say."

His uncle stood before him and grabbed him by the shoulders. He leaned toward him and said, "Tell me the truth, Benny. That's what I want. We'll deal with it."

Benny could smell the alcohol on his uncle's breath. And he could see the strain in his eyes.

"Okay, I'll tell you," Benny said. "Just hear me out all the way before you kick my ass, okay?"

Uncle Tony relaxed the grip on Benny's shoulders. His face seemed to sag with angst and he uttered, "Oh shit. I don't think I like the sound of that." He took a deep breath, then continued. "Let's go into my office and talk."

They entered the small back room.

The aroma of alcohol hung in the air.

Their talk lasted for over an hour. Benny knew he had no recourse but to tell the truth, so he did. He told Uncle Tony about Gourmet Express. He told him how he'd been ordering extra supplies out of the Franzo's account. He also told him how he had cash hidden in the restaurant to repay the account for the food he had ordered. He told him about how he'd stay late some nights preparing food in the restaurant kitchen for the next day's lunch deliveries. He told him everything, even about his unwilling late-night rendezvous with Ricky.

He had to tell him.

Uncle Tony was family.

Real family.

During the seventy-minute conversation, Benny had watched his uncle suck down three Dewar's. He'd watched him rub his hands over his face and try to suppress the anger he was obviously feeling. He'd seen him begin to cry, then break out in hysterical laughter.

But the thing that touched Benny the most was something entirely different. It was the way Uncle Tony got up from his chair, pulled Benny out of his seat, and hugged him after Benny offered to give him the profits he had made from Gourmet Express.

Benny had said, "I'm just a nobody to guys like Ricky. They'll come after *you* harder. I've seen the way they come in here and bust your balls. What are they gonna do to me? Kick my ass? I'm small potatoes. I don't know what your troubles with them are exactly, Uncle Tony, but they gotta be worse than mine. So you take the money. I can make more."

Uncle Tony released Benny from the embrace. "I don't know, Benny. I can't take your money."

"Why not?"

"We'll work this out, you and me," he said. "Right now, we got a dinner crowd coming in. We'll sleep on this and talk about it tomorrow."

"Okay," Benny agreed. He felt weird. He had always hated being in limbo, but that's where he was now—in more ways than one.

Some customers had already been seated in the dining room, and Uncle Tony walked around to some of them, saying hello and welcome, and shaking hands with others.

Just like nothing had happened.

Just like business as usual. And for the rest of the evening it *was* business as usual.

But Benny knew it wouldn't stay like that for long.

And he was right.

The last diners left the restaurant, and Angelo closed the door behind them and was about to lock up, but before he could complete the task, the door was pushed open from the outside, and three men—including Greco, the accountant—forced their way in.

"Where's the boss?" Greco demanded.

"He just left about ten minutes ago," Angelo answered.

"You're full of shit," Greco said. "Now where is he?"

This time he didn't wait for a response. Instead, he yelled out, "Tony, get your ass out here!"

Benny heard the words from the kitchen. He stopped wrapping up a piece of locatelli and stepped into the dining area to see what the commotion was all about. When he made eye contact with Greco, the hairs on his neck stood straight up.

"Hi, kid," Greco said. "We want to talk to you . . . but we want to talk to your uncle first. He in the back?"

"He went home after the last customers were served," he said.

"Quit fucking around," Greco spat out.

One of Greco's accomplices apparently grew tired of waiting and just marched into the kitchen. Benny stepped aside and let him pass. Then the man opened Tony's office door, flipped on the light, and looked around. Satisfied that he wasn't in there, he opened the side door and peered left and right outside. Then he closed the door and marched past Benny back into the dining room.

"You," Greco snarled, pointing at Angelo, "can get out of here. Put on your coat, quick, and head out."

Then, pointing at Benny, he ordered, "You don't go anywhere."

The door opened behind Greco and a stylishly dressed man in a perfect-fitting navy blue suit entered.

Angelo left through the front door, avoiding eye contact with any of the four men in the restaurant.

Greco said to the man who had just arrived, "He ain't here. But this punk is." He nodded toward Benny.

"I was wondering why you guys were just standing around," the man said. "You can wait in the car. Pete's getting lonely listening to the radio all by himself."

"But . . . ," Greco began to protest.

"Wait in the car," he repeated. "You've done your job. I can take over now."

Although disturbed, Greco did as he was told. Then the man peered at Benny, who he noticed was visibly shaken.

"What's the matter? You scared?"

"Yes, sir," Benny replied.

"You got something to be scared about? You got a guilty conscience or something?"

"No. I mean, I don't think so. No."

"Then what are you scared of?" the man smiled. He looked at the two men with him. "Maybe it's these two guys? Is that it? You feel outnumbered? Intimidated maybe?"

"I guess so."

The man laughed. Then he turned to the other two and said,

"Why don't you guys wait in the car, too? I'll call you if I need you."

The men left without saying a word.

Then it was just Benny and . . . whoever this man was. Benny knew he was going to find that out real soon.

"You got any salad back there in the kitchen?" the man asked.

"Yes, sir," Benny answered.

"Bring me some. There a house dressing for the salad?"

"Sure."

"Bring me some of that too."

Benny went into the kitchen and prepared the salad quickly. He used fresh Boston lettuce, cucumbers, tomatoes, red onions, red peppers, and radishes. He wasn't going to insult his "guest" by giving him stuff that had been sitting around the kitchen for an hour or two.

He poured a few ounces of the dressing into a small cruet, then brought the dish of salad and the cruet to the man who had now taken off his coat and made himself comfortable at a table facing the door.

Benny put the dish, the cruet, and a knife and fork in front of the man.

"Would you care for something to drink?" Benny asked nervously.

"Not right now," the man answered. He nodded at the chair opposite him. "Sit down."

The man poured the dressing on his salad in a circular motion. He stuck a piece of lettuce with the fork and lifted it to his mouth.

"That's real good dressing," he said. "It's different. What's in it?"

Benny rattled off a list of all the ingredients, one of which was crushed mint leaves.

"That's it," the man said. "Mint. Just a hint of it. Very good."

Benny tried to manage a smile. "It's my recipe," he said, not really knowing why.

"Really? You shitting me?"

"No, sir."

"Good," he said, forking more salad into his mouth. "That's exactly what I want."

"I don't think I understand," Benny said.

"I want no bullshitting. No lying. No half truths. No crap. I want the truth, and I want *you* to tell it to me."

Benny gulped. He hoped he hadn't done it audibly.

"So, for starters . . . what the fuck did you think you were getting away with?" the man asked nonchalantly, between mouthfuls of salad.

Benny tried to talk, but found himself stuttering and hemming and hawing.

"I'm not hearing anything," the man said.

Benny took a deep breath and tried to pull himself together. "Sorry."

"So?"

"So . . . ," Benny began, "let me just tell you that I haven't stolen any money."

"Really? There seems to be some difference of opinion about that. Especially to my accountant, who I think you've met."

"You mean Greco?" Benny asked. Then he corrected himself. "I mean, *Mr.* Greco."

"Yeah, Mr. Greco."

"He's my uncle's accountant, too."

"That right?" the man asked, finishing the last bite of the salad and wiping his lips with a napkin. "Let me tell you something. Greco's your uncle's accountant because I asked him to be your uncle's accountant. Greco works for me. You understand what I'm saying?"

Benny thought he understood but said nothing for fear of saying the wrong thing.

"Greco tells me there's some fishy shit going on in this place. Crates of *crawfish* for one. And more stock in the kitchen than this place will sell before it goes bad. You know something about that, don't you?"

Benny trembled just a little. "Yeah."

"So," the man continued, leaning forward. "Tell me."

Benny had no choice but to come clean with his whole story. He gave his assurances that there was no embezzling going on, no money lost from his uncle's business. He was as careful as he could be to leave out the names of his friends—particularly Joey Arso—who had helped him with his scheme. Nor did the man ask for the names of any accomplices.

He just listened silently, only once interrupting Benny when he asked for a glass of water, which Benny promptly got for him.

Then he continued his story, telling the man about how Gourmet Express had grown faster than he ever thought possible.

The man asked Benny why he was doing all this. Was it just to make some quick money? Did he hope to start a legitimate food business?

Benny had told the truth so far, so he decided to go all the way. If this man was going to break his legs, or worse, he would do it anyway. So Benny told him that the sharks were into him for a few grand. He added that they were into his uncle, he thought, for a whole lot more. His first priority was paying off those debts—both his and his uncle's—as soon as he could.

The man just stared at him when Benny finished what he had to say.

"Do you know who you're talking to?" the man asked.

"No," Benny answered honestly. He wondered if he should know. Would the man be insulted because he *didn't* know?

"You can call me Mr. Lacerra. Your uncle knows who I am. He knows very well." Mr. Lacerra finished drinking the glass of water, then continued. "Well, that was an interesting story. Should I believe you?"

Benny said, "Yes. It's the truth."

"You been dealing with Ricky, same guy your uncle deals with?"

"Yes, sir."

"And Napoli too, I understand."

"Yes, sir."

"How much you owe them?"

"I think a little over five thousand."

"You got it?"

"Just about. Last I counted it, it was about thirty-eight hundred dollars. It might be four thousand dollars."

"And you made all that through your deliveries?"

"Yes, sir."

"You got it on you?"

"It's in the kitchen."

"That's not a good place for it."

"No, I guess not."

"Give it to me."

"What?"

"I said give it to me. Go get it."

Benny walked into the kitchen, retrieved a cigar box he had shoved under the refrigerator, and returned to the table. He handed it to Mr. Lacerra.

"You can sit down again," he said.

Mr. Lacerra opened the box, held the cash, mostly fifty-dollar bills, in his hand, and flipped the edges. "Yeah," he said, "looks like about four G's."

Benny fidgeted in his seat. He suddenly realized he was soaked in sweat.

"So here's the deal, my friend. Benny, isn't it?"

"Yes, sir."

"You oughta have your fat little fingers cut off and served with ziti. Right?"

Benny didn't answer. He just stared at the table.

"That's if I wanted to go easy on you."

A drop of sweat ran down Benny's nose and dropped onto his chin.

Mr. Lacerra sat back and shoved the wad of bills into his pocket. "But I'm in a good mood tonight. And I gotta tell you, for a young snot nose, you got a lot of balls. You really think you coulda pulled this off forever without getting caught? I don't think so. You also obviously got some know-how and some real—what's the word I'm looking for?—ingenuity. Four G's isn't bad for a small-scale home-grown business like you got. So this is what I'm gonna do."

Benny interrupted. "My uncle didn't know anything about it. I swear to God."

Mr. Lacerra didn't respond to the interruption. "As I was saying, I'm gonna take this money and square you with Ricky and

Napoli. They won't bother you any more for this money. You got me? It's settled. You continue gambling and run up another tab, that's your problem. You fuck up again, you *get* fucked, you know what I mean?"

Benny closed his eyes. Then he said, "I am *so* grateful."

Lacerra continued. "I'm not done yet. You keep on running your food business. I want you to keep records, and I don't mean bullshit records. Accurate ones. No skimming off the top, no horseshit. Can you do that?"

"Yeah. I took an accounting course at St. John's."

"Because if you can't, I can get Greco to help you."

"I can do it," Benny assured him. The last thing he wanted was Greco breathing down his neck.

"Greco's gonna check your records every so often, so they better be straight. You reading me?"

"Yes, sir."

"I get half your profits, payable the first week of every month. You see the other two guys I came in here with? One or both of them will visit you the first Friday every month. You have that fifty percent in cash for them."

"I understand."

"You sure you understand?"

"Yes, sir."

"You understand that from now on you work for me? That half—at least for now—of your business is mine."

"Yes."

"Good," Lacerra said, leaning forward on the table. "You got any questions?"

Benny thought for a moment, then said, "Just one . . . if you don't mind me asking."

"I just asked *you* if you had a question."

"What about my uncle?"

"What about him?"

"I was going to use that money to help *him* out first."

Lacerra stared at Benny. He was silent for a moment. "You're loyal to your family. I like that. I really like that. Just remember that from now on you're part of another, much larger family. And that same loyalty must be there at all times. You know what I'm talking about, don't you?"

"Yes, sir."

"I'm doing you a major favor here. You owe me. You owe me big time." He pointed a finger directly between Benny's eyes. "And I'm taking a chance on you, who I don't even really know, and that's something I don't normally do, because big risks are what get people fucked over. You better never let me down, Benny. Never!"

"No, sir," Benny managed to say. "I won't. You have my word."

Lacerra stood up and buttoned his coat. Benny stood up when he did.

"I'll see what I can do to take some of the heat off your uncle," he added. "No promises, though."

"Thank you."

Lacerra headed for the door, but before he opened it to leave, he said, "You really make that salad dressing?"

"Yes, sir," Benny replied.

"It was real good. And the taste sorta lingers in your mouth. You do most of the cooking here?"

"I do most of it now. And there are others. Uncle Tony does some too."

"Maybe I'll start eating here more often. You'll cook for me, right?"

"Sure."

"You make a good Bolognese sauce?"

"I haven't had any complaints. Everybody seems to think it's good."

"Well, maybe I'll come in personally every month. You can cook me up something special."

"It would be my honor," Benny said. And when he saw the reaction in Lacerra's face—like he had said *exactly* the right thing—he finally calmed down a bit.

"See ya, Benny," Lacerra said as he exited. "Don't fuck up now, you hear me?"

"I hear you," he said as the door closed behind Lacerra. "And thank you."

Benny headed for the kitchen, carrying his now empty cigar box.

Then he leaned on a counter and caught his breath.

Salad

—

Blood oranges & anchovies with pine nuts over Boston Bibb lettuce

— Blood Orange & Anchovy Salad —

In a bowl, whisk anchovies, shallots, Dijon mustard, red wine vinegar, sugar, a few splashes of blood-orange juice.
Pour over Bibb lettuce, then garnish with orange slices, pine nuts, and yellow and red grape tomatoes.

∽ Third Course: Salad ∽

Forget about music.

Benny knew that *food* was the way to soothe the savage beast.

Since he had served his crawfish bisque, the bickering between the men outside had almost completely ceased. He was amazed at how quiet the place got while they were eating. There had been hardly a sound except for a slurp here or a cough there.

Then, as the guys finished up, Benny stepped into the dining area to collect the dishes. He was beginning to get tired. He wasn't used to doing *all* the work: cooking, serving, even acting as busboy. And the night was still young, and there were several more courses to go. But this was what he had been told to do, so he simply *did* it.

For some reason, the men had begun talking about the movies. The tone of this discussion had shifted to one that was much more lighthearted than the previous ones. Maybe, Benny thought, they were simply trying to relieve the pressure they were undoubtedly feeling, the pressure of not really knowing why they were here at this restaurant on this night.

"*The Godfather*," Palumbo said. "There can't be a better movie on *la famiglia* than *The Godfather*."

"The first two parts, at least," Ischia said. "That third one was a fucking disaster."

"Pacino was still good, though."

"Yeah," Apromonte interjected, "but even *The Godfather* doesn't get it right, you know?"

"No movie gets it completely right," Ianello said. "Not even *Goodfellas*."

"Now that fucking movie still pisses me off," Pally said. "Glorifying that rat scumbag."

"You think it glorifies him?" Di Pietro asked. "I don't think so. I think Hill comes off as a lowlife loser."

"It still treats him better than he should've been."

Abbazio said, "But what about all the *really bad* movies? You remember *The Valachi Papers*? I haven't seen that one in twenty years. Not on television. Not on videotape. Not on DVD. Nowhere."

"Somebody burned all the fucking prints," Pally stated. "I hope."

Benny removed the last of the dishes from the table. He added his own comment. "I kinda like *Once Upon a Time in America*. At least it was different. Not the usual stereotypes."

Pally responded, "I can't make it through that whole goddamn movie. Too fucking long! Some douche bag from some artsy-fartsy film school must've made that one. Who the fuck can follow it?"

"It was made by an *Italian*, Sergio Leone," Abbazio corrected. "I think he's the guy who made all those westerns in Italy. You know, the ones with Clint Eastwood."

"*Italian* or not," Pally said, "the guy's still a douche bag."

"I *still* kinda like it," Benny said. "I like the Eastwood westerns too."

Abbazio suddenly let out a loud laugh, and everyone turned toward him.

"Jesus, Benny, I just remembered something," he said.

"What's that?" Benny inquired, still holding a soup dish.

"I guess it was the mideighties," he added. "You and me snuck into a theater on Eighteenth Avenue to see a Clint Eastwood double feature. It was one of the Dirty Harry pictures and some other thing he made . . . something with a monkey in it."

Benny laughed. "Yeah, I remember. We picked up a couple of girls that night."

"We did?" Double A asked. "I don't remember that."

"I'm not surprised," Benny said. "I think you were loaded on PCP."

"Was I? I don't doubt it. The memory cells are fucking gone. I can't even remember the name of that theater, and we used to go there all the time. It was a cinch to sneak into."

Benny remembered. "The Walker. I think it was the Walker."

Di Pietro asked, "This is all very nostalgic, I must say. But I'm still hungry."

Benny shot a nasty look at Di Pietro, then softened its impact by saying, "Well, since you guys are talking movies, maybe you'd like some popcorn for the next course?"

No one answered, so Benny said, "Okay, then. I'll get the salad."

"What is it, a Caesar salad?" Aspromonte asked.

Benny stared at him and smirked. "It's blood oranges, anchovies, and pine nuts over crisp Bibb lettuce."

"Huh?" Aspromonte uttered, revealing his limited knowledge of food and even more limited food choice experience.

"Trust me," Benny said. "Caesar would've given up his empire for a salad like this."

Then he headed for the kitchen, wondering whether some of these guys would ever get past the spaghetti and Caesar salad stage and start to develop a taste for some of the less common dishes out there.

Benny's Gourmet Express business outgrew its somewhat "hidden" location. Its customer base continued to expand, as did its staff and the number of items on its menu. It got to the point where, clearly, another kitchen and at least a storefront were necessary. And since there was really no need to keep the operation of the business hidden any longer, Benny rented a small rundown store on Thirteenth Avenue that had once been a Chinese takeout place.

He sank some of his own money into renovating it, but, in actuality, it didn't need that much refurbishing. Benny invested in a couple of ovens, many pots, pans, and utensils, and gave the place a quick makeover with paint and paneling he and Joey Arso purloined from the local Pergament's. There already was a counter in the place, so he let that stand untouched, except for a cleanup of all the years of grease that had accumulated from the Chinese joint.

He didn't even need to invest in tables or chairs since this was strictly a food delivery business. Maybe, someday soon, Benny thought, he could graduate to that.

He was sure he would.

Not surprisingly, Benny had risen to head chef at Franzo's, and although he took a lot of ribbing about it, he and most of the place's regulars knew it wasn't because of nepotism. No, Benny knew he was a damn good chef. He had all the right qualities: ambition, knowledge, technique, and a certain amount of daring. His uncle pretty much left him on his own as far as the cuisine, although Benny had to promise not to abandon the classic recipes the place was known for.

Benny had no problem with that. Each week at Franzo's he would try at least two new "specials," totally his own ideas. Most of the time they went over; occasionally one would misfire or Benny's reach would exceed his grasp and the experiment would go too wild for the modest neighborhood restaurant.

But people were talking.

Talking about Franzo's.

Talking about the chef.

For over a year it seemed as if everyone was happy.

Benny was still gambling, but he knew better than to get in over his head again. He kept it all on a sane level. Sometimes he'd be up. Other times he'd lose a couple of hundred. But he made sure he always had the means to get any money he might owe a bookie.

And he had become something of a master betting "middles" and winning two ways on basically the same sports bet—a system Angelo had explained to him—so financially he usually was in the black.

Even Uncle Tony was smiling during that time. Benny had helped get Ricky off his back, although Ricky would still come around every so often when his uncle had a new debt to be paid. Mr. Lacerra had kept his word about that. He also kept his word about coming into Franzo's more often. Benny always greeted him when he arrived, treated him like royalty, and handed him the envelope containing his cut on time. Before too long, Benny was able to just about free his uncle of his gambling debt entirely. All from Gourmet Express and the increase in business at Franzo's.

Benny began to note that more connected local figures started eating at the restaurant. He had no doubt that Mr. Lacerra was spreading the good word about Benny. And not just about his abilities in the kitchen. Perhaps about his, what? reliability?

At any rate, Benny began dividing his time between Franzo's and the Thirteenth Avenue storefront. He was always working. He'd hired a few more people to help in the kitchen and with the deliveries, but the bulk of the cooking was still done by him, while Joey Arso managed the phones, the deliveries, and the scheduling of the delivery guys.

He was working his ass off and had little time for much else. He would take a night or an afternoon off here and there, but Gourmet Express was his baby, and other than Joey once in a while, he didn't like leaving it in the hands of a babysitter.

Then, on a sunny July afternoon, Mr. Lacerra had twelve crates of shrimp and four large wooden barrels of black olives brought into the back room of Gourmet Express.

Joey was in charge of the place just then. Benny had left about a half hour earlier to bring home a prescription to his mother, whose diabetes was getting worse as her age increased.

Benny returned just as Mr. Lacerra was getting back in his car. It was the first time he had ever seen Mr. Lacerra without a suit jacket on. Instead, he was wearing a light-blue running suit with the name Sergio Tacchini misspelled in the logo.

"Benny!" Lacerra said jovially when he spotted him. "Just the man I wanted to talk to."

Inside the storefront Benny could see that Joey was acting confused. His friend kept peering into the back.

"Hi, Mr. Lacerra," Benny said. "Did you come in to place an order?"

Lacerra laughed. "Yeah," he answered. "Yeah, you might say that."

He opened the back door of the black Cadillac Seville. "Get in for a minute, Benny. I want to talk to you."

Benny did as he was instructed, sliding all the way over to the passenger side of the backseat. Lacerra slid in beside him.

"Everything okay?" Benny asked.

Lacerra slapped him on the shoulder, as if they were old goombahs. "Yeah, everything's great." He leaned forward and said to the man who was sitting behind the wheel, "Drive around a little bit. We don't want Benny's place getting a bad reputation now, do we?" Then he and the driver laughed.

The car pulled out into the Thirteenth Avenue traffic and he continued. "Benny, I've been thinking. I gotta be honest with you. I think you've done a great job with this place and your uncle's joint. I feel like I was *so* right about you that night we had our first little talk . . . even though I took a lot of shit for it from some of my superiors."

"Sorry," Benny said.

"Don't be sorry," Lacerra returned. "It was fucking worth it. You're squared away, we're both making a profit, and there's been no hitches at all. At least I don't think there has . . ."

He was leaving the way open for Benny to say if there *had* been any. But Benny said nothing because there was nothing to say.

"The cops ever bother you?"

"No," Benny replied. "Not really."

"Not really? That mean they have . . . a little?"

"No. Some cop came in and wanted to see the food license one time. That's all."

"You showed him the one I got for you?"

"Yeah. It worked like a charm. Then I gave him an order of peppers and sausage. And that was the end of it."

"Okay. Anyway, here's what I wanted to tell you. I want you to expand your business a little."

Benny was surprised. "You do? How?"

"I want you to handle some food I've got my hands on, and I'll probably continue to get my hands on."

"You mean you want me to prepare it for you?"

"No," Lacerra corrected, looking Benny straight in the eyes. "I want you to handle it for me."

Benny stared back at him. He didn't know how to answer.

"You know what I'm talking about, right?" Lacerra asked.

"I think so."

"I want you to unload the stuff at restaurants, food markets, wherever. You get a fifteen . . . ah, fuck it . . . we'll make it a twenty percent cut. I'll even give you the names of some people I've done business with before. You know, a list of my clientele. To get you started."

"I understand," Benny said, somewhat timidly.

Lacerra sensed the timidity. "Whatsamatter, Benny? You aren't uncomfortable with this, are you?"

"No, I don't think so."

"Well, don't be uncomfortable. The whole thing is a piece of cake. It's quick, it's easy, it's over. You just gotta be cool about it."

Benny nodded.

"Besides . . . ," Lacerra added, ". . . you owe me, remember?"

Benny remembered. He wouldn't have told Lacerra "no" even if he wanted to.

"I don't have a problem with it," Benny said. "What kind of stuff do I move?"

Lacerra laughed. "Whatever falls off the ships or trucks at the Navy Yard or in Newark or wherever I can get my hands on it."

Benny smiled. "I hear you."

"Good."

Lacerra told the driver to head back to Thirteenth Avenue. "There's shrimp and olives in the back of your place now. That shrimp, in particular, you gotta move fast. But I don't have to tell you that. *You* know shrimp! At least how to serve them in a diavolo sauce. You're really something in the kitchen, I gotta hand you that. The stuff you make at your uncle's is as good as anything I've had in Manhattan."

"Thank you."

"You play ball with me, Benny, you're gonna hit a grand slam one of these days. You'll see."

"I appreciate that."

"Of course, you'll keep records of the transactions you do for me."

"Of course."

The car pulled in front of the modest Gourmet Express storefront. Lacerra reached into his pocket, pulled out a slip of paper, and handed it to Benny.

"Those are some people you can fence the stuff to. Tell them I sent you. Then they shouldn't give you any shit. If they do, you let me know. There's prices listed there for a box of shrimp and for the olives. You buy food. Those prices okay?"

"They're cheaper than most I've seen. I should have no trouble selling them at these prices."

"Okay, Benny, get out of my car and get to work. I'm heading for Breezy Point. Can't you tell?" He tugged at his shirt. "Is this some outfit or what? The beach! The sun! The Silver Gull! Shit, I need this day."

"Enjoy yourself," Benny said.

"I will. There's a barmaid at that place who's double-jointed and very flexible. . . . Well, you get the picture."

Benny said good-bye again and closed the car door.

The Cadillac made a U-turn and headed for the entrance to the Belt Parkway on Fourteenth Avenue.

So Benny began fencing shrimp that same evening.

He brought it personally to the manager of a restaurant on Fort Hamilton Parkway, near the entrance to the Verrazano Bridge. At first the manager was going to throw Benny out in the street on his ass, but when Benny mentioned Mr. Lacerra, the man's attitude changed completely. He immediately took three boxes of shrimp and paid Benny what he asked. He even asked if Benny would be back soon with more.

"Yeah," he answered. "I'm not sure when, though."

"I understand," the manager said. "Can I get you a glass of wine before you go?"

Benny was beginning to enjoy being treated like someone of importance. "No, thanks. I have another couple more stops to make."

Benny unloaded all but one of the crates of shrimp that night.

That one he kept for Franzo's and for Gourmet Express. After all, the price *was* less than he could get the shrimp for, and he didn't think Mr. Lacerra would mind, as long as the money was accounted for.

He unloaded the olives the next day. Early in the morning, he and Joey Arso visited a few fruit and vegetable places on Eighty-sixth Street, near Bay Parkway. The grocers were also names on the list that had been given to him.

And that was that.

Lacerra was right.

It was quick, it was easy, and it was over.

Mission accomplished, cash collected and accounted for.

And Benny would be pocketing one fifth of it.

Benny knew he could get used to this sort of action real easily.

And he did.

At least twice a week, Lacerra or his men would drop off all kinds of stuff. Sometimes it was shrimp; sometimes it was tomatoes or other produce; and once in a while it was something out of the ordinary like caviar or truffles.

Whatever it was, Benny had no trouble unloading the stuff. He slowly added names to the customer list Lacerra had given him. Benny made a few contacts of his own; in fact, as his reputation as a chef grew and blossomed, he made the acquaintance of many restaurant owners from Brooklyn and other parts of the city.

Benny was becoming something of a minor celebrity, and a go-to guy in "food fencing." And with that celebrity and the growing sums of money he was making from his various ventures, he was feeling very confident and very independent.

The feeling of confidence was a good thing that would serve him well.

The feeling of independence, on the other hand, wouldn't.

Somewhere down the line, Benny must have slacked off in the record-keeping or laid out some cash he forgot to record. There was a gaping hole in the numbers, and the balance was not in Benny's favor. Maybe it had been a mistake, Benny surmised, to start fencing other hijacked food that he came across from other sources, food that Mr. Lacerra most likely knew nothing about. Someone, somewhere, must have fucked him over. Benny wished he was a better bookkeeper than he actually was.

He was able to cover the loss for now, but Benny knew that he'd better raise the missing money before too long. He knew he'd have to come up with some scheme to do that.

And he did.

Even though it was Joey Arso who actually inspired the idea.

One morning, when Benny showed up at Gourmet Express, he noticed Joey standing in the back with a big shit-eating grin on his face. Joey was twirling a key ring on his forefinger.

"What's up with you?" Benny asked, knowing that something had to be very right or very wrong. "You look like the cat that ate the canary."

"Nah," Joey said. "But I *do* have something to show you."

"Yeah? What?"

"Check this out."

Joey removed a coarse blanket that covered about two dozen large cans of olive oil. Benny looked closely at the brand name.

"That stuff is shit," he noted. "Did Mr. Lacerra bring that in?"

"Nope," Joey answered.

"So where'd it come from?"

"I got it last night."

"You got it how? Where?"

"Some truck down near Atlantic Avenue," Joey explained. "I had to drive my cousin down there to buy some bread—you know, that good pita bread they bake down there in the Arab section. My uncle wanted it, the fuckin' Syrian asshole. The guy my aunt Maria married. That guy who has the real estate office in Sunset Park."

"Yeah, I know who you mean."

"So my cousin Anna goes into the bakery to get the bread and whatever the hell else she had to get. Meanwhile, I'm sitting in the car, waiting. And waiting. And waiting. And I notice that the whole time there's this truck parked on the side street with the back open, and nobody around. I mean nobody. So I get out of the car and take a look in the back. Tons of these cans of oil. So I grab some and throw them in the trunk of my car."

Benny shook his head in disbelief. "You took all this in broad daylight? All by yourself?"

"No and yes."

"What?"

"It was getting dark, so not really in daylight. But yeah, all by myself. Two at a time."

"You're a fucking nut, Joey, you know that?"

Joey shrugged his shoulders. "Maybe. But look at all this olive oil I got for nothing. Twenty-four huge cans of the shit. For nothing. You won't have to order oil for half a year."

Benny shook his head again. "I wouldn't lube my fucking car with that crap," he said. "But I appreciate your motive, man, I really do."

"So you can't use it?" Joey asked.

"Oh, I'll find a use for it," Benny said. "I just won't cook with it. Some of those Arab restaurants don't give a shit what they use.

They're used to this stuff. They pour it on their hummus and stir it in. But I won't use it for my stuff."

"Hey, sorry," Joey said.

Benny could see that Joey's feelings were hurt. He put his arm around his friend's neck. "Hey, man, you did good. You did fine. The stuff will come in handy, I'm sure."

"Yeah, okay," Joey said. "Maybe you can fence it when we're bringing Mr. Lacerra's stuff around."

"I don't know," Benny replied. "Not too many guys will go for this cheap stuff."

Then an idea hit Benny.

"But they might go for it if they thought it was top-notch stuff."

"Huh?" Joey uttered.

"We can pull a switch. Take this stuff and put it in other containers."

"Think we can pull that off?"

"We can try. We just got to be careful," Benny said. "In the meantime, do me a favor and stick those cans back in your car trunk. I don't want Mr. Lacerra seeing them. Know what I mean?"

"Sure," Joey answered. "Ain't his stuff. Don't want him getting pissed off."

"Or even suspicious," Benny added.

A few minutes later, the cans were weighing down the trunk of Joey's black '77 Celica.

For the rest of that day, both at Gourmet Express and Franzo's, Benny poured the fine oil used at those places into any containers and bottles he could get ahold of. Then he collected all the empty containers, stuck them in a black plastic trash bag, and put them in the trunk of his car.

Benny also had Joey Arso go through supermarket circulars, find any who were having big sales on high-grade olive oil, and then go to those supermarkets and buy the lowest-priced top-of-the-line oil he could get. He told him to buy as much as the stores would let him have. (And he gave him a list of the best brand names.)

That day, Joey visited all the local food markets. Several Key Food stores. The big Pathmark store over on Sixty-fifth Street. The Grand Union. Smaller, local, non-chain supermarkets. By the end of the afternoon Joey had a couple of dozen bottles and cans of good olive oil. They too resided in his car trunk.

Benny also ordered a large quantity of high-end, extra-virgin olive oil from his usual suppliers. But he ordered it in smaller bottles than he normally would. It would be more than enough to cover the delivery business and Franzo's and would leave him a good supply left over. Not to mention the use—the *reuse*—of the bottles.

Benny wondered if he'd been stupid to get some of the oil from the supermarkets. But then he thought about it, and ultimately he thought it was a good idea. He didn't want all of the good stuff to come from the same sources. And the oil from the supermarkets would be harder—in fact, all but impossible—to trace.

When, in a day or two, Benny had large quantities of the various quality oils, he began his operation. He and Joey spent hours, working well into the small hours of the morning, performing the operation.

They called it "doing transfusions."

The high-quality containers were filled with much cheaper stuff and were resealed with great care. And the high-end olive oil was stored in any containers Benny could get his hands on. He could use the good oil at Gourmet Express and at Franzo's, even if it was stored in odd containers. No one would know except him and Joey. He had so much of it, he brought some to his parents and other members of his family. Joey took some home also. He even sent some to his cousin for her Arab father.

Benny continued to make his usual rounds, distributing the repackaged oil to his usual yet ever expanding list of customers. There were a few, of course, that he wouldn't sell the oil to. These were guys who knew their food and supplies better than the usual guys at local restaurants and pizzerias. Or they were guys who were *very* connected, and Benny felt that it wasn't worth the risk to play around with them.

All he needed was wind of this getting back to someone at the top.

So for a while the deals went down, and Benny managed to pass off the inferior oil to many of his customers. He rarely heard a complaint from anyone, though on the few occasions when he did, he just said there must have been a screwup somewhere and took it back. Or he said he'd mention it to his source. His customers, of course, thought that source was Mr. Lacerra . . . and others farther up the organization.

So they rarely said a word in complaint.

Both Benny and Joey were beginning to show signs of wear and tear. Neither was sleeping much, and both were always running around somewhere. Even Benny's uncle Tony, who knew nothing of the "transfusions" and whose restaurant was spared the low-quality oil, told Benny he should take a vacation.

But Benny knew that until he'd filled in that financial hole in his books, he'd better press on, doing what he had to, no matter what it took. Or the vacation he took might be the permanent kind.

He *had*, so far, been able to hide any deficit from Lacerra. Benny had been giving him the money he should have been. He wasn't negligent with the payments; he wasn't even late with them. And the gap *was* closing. The financial hole was getting much smaller, even though the extra work was depriving him of sleep and almost completely killed any social life.

It was temporary, Benny told himself. Just a while longer and everything will be okay again. Then, maybe, he'd take a vacation. Italy, maybe. Or to some other, more exotic place, where he might be able to partake in a new—at least to him—cuisine.

That vacation was still a way off, he knew. But he began to think about it more often, perhaps as a way of relieving the stress he was feeling. He just wanted to square the books. That's all. And he was getting it done, but it seemed to be taking forever.

One afternoon, when one of Mr. Lacerra's guys showed up for the boss's cut, he asked Benny if he could recommend a truly great bottle of wine. He said he wanted to impress "a rich broad."

Benny asked him what food they'd be eating with the wine.

The man said he wasn't sure. He wasn't sure that they'd be eating food at all with it. He just wanted to impress the broad.

Benny wrote him a list of various types of wines and the meals they best complemented. He also listed a few fine wines that were great with or without food.

"What are they called? Sitting around wines?" he asked.

"Yeah," Benny laughed. "You can call them that if you want to. Some of these wines aren't cheap."

"No problem," the bill collector answered. "Getting into this broad's pants will be worth it."

"I hear you," Benny said, handing him the list. "Good luck."

That's when Benny thought about yet another form of transfusion. And speeding up the end of his financial shortfall.

If he could pull off the switch with olive oil . . . why not with wine?

Why the hell not?

When he told Joey Arso his idea, Joey ran his fingers through his hair and let out a deep breath. "And when are we gonna have the time to do all this, Benny? I think it's a good idea and all that, but Christ, man, how much can we do?"

Benny knew he had been pushing his friend hard, and he felt bad about it. "Look, man, I'll make it worth your while."

Joey brushed the statement aside with a wave of his hand. "I know that. I ain't worried about that. I just don't see how we can manage everything. Benny, we're gonna need more time to do it all. And we're gonna need more help, more people."

He was right, Benny knew. He'd have to start taking some time off, at least here and there, from Franzo's. His uncle Tony wouldn't have too much of a problem with that. After all, hadn't he suggested that Benny go on vacation? So that was workable.

But Benny did *not* particularly want to get more people involved in Gourmet Express, and *definitely* did not want to get more people involved in the transfusions.

After he thought about it for a while, though, he told Joey to hire another delivery guy and someone else who had some smarts and some personality and a good phone manner to help Joey handle the coordination of the orders and deliveries. And, he emphasized, someone who could be trusted completely.

Joey said his cousin Mark could use the job.

Benny wasn't that surprised.

Though he didn't know Mark, Benny was aware that most of the people working at Gourmet Express were Joey's relatives. His little brother. A couple of other cousins. But Benny didn't mind. They had all worked out so far, and he was happy to keep his business—legitimate or otherwise—within the scope of one big, happy family. And Joey *was* family. At least almost.

Benny gave Joey the go-ahead. Then, after meeting the new hires and feeling satisfied with them, the wine transfusions began.

The wine transfusions went every bit as smoothly as the olive oil deals. In fact, it got to the point where Benny was offering special deals on combination orders. From day to day, Benny's offerings would change, although the wine became a constant, just as the oil had. Benny was savvy enough not to switch real bottom-of-the-barrel wine with top brands. His transfusions were much more subtle and performed with lots of thought and real artistry. They had to be; the last thing he wanted was to get caught. Even the corking of the bottles and the resealing was performed with artistry. Although it wasn't perfect, only someone who might be looking for them would notice the imperfections of Benny's and Joey's repackaging.

"Jesus," Benny said after looking at the first batch of bottles. "You can't tell one wine from another by looking at them."

Lacerra, meanwhile, would drop off whatever he had and he thought Benny could move for him. There was a variety of foods: cheeses, seafood, chickens on occasion. And Benny moved what he could—which most of the time was most of the stuff—and used the rest himself, often creating new specials at Franzo's based on whatever food he had left over from Lacerra's deliveries.

It seemed everyone was happy. Lacerra was getting his payments; Benny's uncle's restaurant was thriving to the point where

Benny now had two assistant chefs working with and for him; and Benny was only a few hundred dollars short of making up his financial deficit. Even Joey Arso was happy, even though he was working more hours since he started with Benny than he had ever worked in his whole life.

Then one afternoon Mr. Lacerra came into Franzo's for a late lunch. The place wasn't very busy, so he asked Benny to sit with him. Benny told one of the assistant chefs what to do for the next half hour or so, removed his chef's garb, and joined Lacerra at the table.

"Benny," Lacerra said right away, "I need you to do me a favor. You don't mind, do you?"

"No. What is it?"

"Do you know the name Vito Famighetti?"

"Can't say I do, no."

"Well, he's . . . how do I put this? . . . like a lieutenant, know what I mean? And he's very close to Mr. Ranallo, you know? Leo's dad."

"Okay."

"So here's the problem, and I thought you might be the perfect person to help," Lacerra said, sitting back in the chair. "The other night I'm in the social club playing poker with a bunch of the guys, and in walks Mr. Ranallo and Famighetti. Well, Famighetti's squawking and carrying on how he ate dinner at this place on Kings Highway, and the food was so bad, he almost puked it up."

Benny leaned forward, listening intently. He knew most of the places on Kings Highway. Some of them were restaurants he was fencing Mr. Lacerra's goods to. Some were purchasing Benny's "transfused" oil and wine.

"So Mr. Ranallo turns to me and asks me if I know the place. Café Bari. Of course, I know the place. I think it was one of the places I put on my customer list that I gave to you."

"That's right," Benny nodded. "It was. Seems like a good enough place. It's clean, I can tell you that."

"Well, then that ain't the problem." Mr. Lacerra stabbed some ziti with his fork and continued. "Anyhow, Mr. Ranallo asks me— since he knows I'm moving food to various places—to see if I can find out what's wrong at the place. What the hell's going on, you know?"

Benny forked a piece of mozzarella with fresh tomato into his mouth.

"But, hey, let's face it, Benny. I like good food, and most of the time I can tell a good melon from a rotten one. In some of the work I do, I *better* be able to do that much, you know? But shit, I'm no gourmet, though I gotta tell you this marinara is wonderful, though I expect no less than that from you."

"Thanks."

"So here's the deal. I need you to go over to Café Bari sometime real soon."

"What do you want me to do?"

"I don't know," Mr. Lacerra answered. "Check the place out. See what kind of stuff they're using. See if the cooking staff knows what the hell they're doing. Maybe give them some pointers. Whatever you can do."

"Will they be expecting me?" Benny asked. "My guess is they won't appreciate me just barging in and lording it over them."

"Oh, yeah, no problem with that," Lacerra replied. "I sort of told them someone would be stopping by. You can do this for me, can't you?"

Benny knew that, despite the niceties of the conversation, he really didn't have a choice. "Sure. Is tomorrow afternoon okay?"

Lacerra finished his ziti and washed it down with the rest of his Coke with lemon. "That would be perfect. I'll talk to you the day after that. You can let me know what the deal is."

The two men shook hands. Mr. Lacerra left Franzo's pleased, and Benny returned to the kitchen, a nervous knot forming in his stomach.

Oh shit, he thought. This might get . . . complicated.

When he arrived at Café Bari at 2:30 the next afternoon, the manager recognized him but was surprised that Benny was the person that Lacerra had suggested would come by. And he didn't seem at all pleased.

"*You're* who they send?" Alfonso De Cresenzo, the manager, asked.

"Why, who were you expecting?" Benny asked sarcastically, not at all appreciating the manager's tone of voice. "James Fucking Beard?"

De Cresenzo responded, "Hey, I know you're a favorite of the big guys—right now. And if Mr. Lacerra sent you, so be it. Look around, inspect the kitchen, question the staff, do whatever you want. Just don't take any attitude with me."

"Attitude?" Benny repeated. "Me? I just got here. *You* drop the attitude and we'll just get this done. Or do you have a problem with that?"

"No, no problem."

So Benny checked the place out. He looked over their supplies—quickly—since he was more than familiar with some of them. De Cresenzo had been purchasing Benny's inferior "transfused" olive oil and quite a bit of other supplies. A whole lot of the stuff they were using to prepare their meals *was* substandard—or at least not top quality.

A lot of the stuff they had Benny would never use . . . even if he was willing to fence it.

He tried to be both unobtrusive and confident. He gave the chef, a man in his forties who was obviously *not* schooled in the culinary arts, a few pointers. Benny was easy on the guy; he didn't hold it against him that he was probably somebody's cousin or uncle and not really a professionally trained chef. After all, Benny himself didn't have any real schooling in that area either, except for his own home schooling and on-the-job training. So Benny didn't talk to him like some snob.

He also briefly "interviewed" a pretty young waitress who worked there. He had noticed her great looks and beautiful reddish-brown hair the moment he had entered the place. But he put off talking to her until he was finished with the other staff members.

When he felt it *was* time to talk to her, he approached her. She was sitting at a table going over receipts. Benny noticed how gorgeous her crossed legs were under the table.

"Excuse me," Benny said. "May I talk to you for a moment?"

"Sure," she said, looking up at him with her deep brown eyes. "Have a seat."

"Thanks," he said, sitting down.

"I saw you before, looking around in the kitchen," she said. "You from the Board of Health or something?"

"No, not exactly," he smiled. "I just work for one of the partners who has a percentage of this and a couple of other restaurants."

She shot him a look of concern. It highlighted her cheekbones. "There's nothing wrong, I hope."

"Nothing to worry about," Benny said. He noticed De Cresenzo talking to someone outside the restaurant. "I was just wondering if you get many complaints from your customers."

"About me?" she asked nervously.

Benny smiled.

God, she was gorgeous, he thought. And what he suspected was a hint of a Southern accent made her even more attractive. "Now how could anyone in his right mind complain about you?"

She smiled back, recognizing the compliment. "Well, thanks. But I'm serious. Has somebody complained about me?"

"Not at all. I'm referring to the meals, the cuisine. Please be honest with me if there have been complaints. They're not a reflection on you in any way."

She smiled again, but looked outside and she too saw De Cresenzo smoking a cigarette, killing time outside the restaurant talking to a local shopkeeper.

"This won't get back to . . ."

Before she even finished the question, Benny assured her it wouldn't.

"Yeah, there have been some complaints recently," she answered. "And I'm usually the one who has to deal with them."

"Tell me," Benny urged her on.

"Well, sometimes the customers tell me something tastes funny or the meat isn't tender. And a couple of times I've noticed the cooks watering down some of the sauces in the back. Although maybe they're supposed to do that. I don't know. I'm no cook, believe me. God, I could mess up a grilled cheese sandwich. And sometimes some of the customers complain that the fish tastes too . . . I don't know . . . fishy, I guess."

"Yeah, that's a common complaint," Benny answered. "Usually when a place keeps the fish around too long or buys fish that isn't as fresh as it should be, or perhaps doesn't take the time to really clean their pans after each use. But you don't get that complaint very often in a place that cares about the preparation and presentation of its food. Anything else?"

"Look, Mr. . . ."

"Lacoco," Benny smiled. "Ben Lacoco."

"Mr. Lacoco, then," she continued. "I really don't want to get myself fired, if you know what I mean."

Benny knew he had some ammunition now in case De Cresenzo acted up again. So he rose from the table, gently shook her hand, and said, "I understand perfectly. You have nothing to worry about, I assure you, Miss . . ."

"Vaughn. Teena Vaughn."

"Miss Vaughn. I hope we meet again sometime."

Benny felt just a bit lightheaded. He knew he'd been momentarily dazzled by this Southern belle.

When the feeling faded and he felt he had done what Mr. Lacerra had asked—at least perfunctorily—he made a few suggestions to De Cresenzo, who was still outside the restaurant, now alone. These suggestions seemed to reinsert the bug up the manager's ass.

"I got a few ideas of my own, you know," he said to Benny. "Like maybe some of the shit I've been getting from you and your goofy friend ain't as good as it's supposed to be."

"What's that supposed to mean?" Benny asked, although he had a pretty good idea what the man meant.

"Like ever since I switched my brand of oil—upgrading, I

thought—I get some complaints about how some of our dishes taste heavy and greasy. How the aftertaste stays with you for hours."

"Who's said that?" Benny asked.

"Lots of people."

"Really. Maybe your chef should have a lighter hand with it."

"Or maybe the oil I'm using is flat-out shit."

De Cresenzo's comment struck a nerve in Benny . . . basically because he knew it was true.

"So don't buy it anymore," Benny said bluntly.

"I won't," De Cresenzo confirmed.

"Fine. Talk to Mr. Lacerra about it. You tell him his oil is shit."

The manager silently thought about that proposition for a moment.

"You tell him his oil is shit and that you're not buying it anymore," Benny repeated. "Or maybe I should tell him for you. You want me to do that? I can do that. No problem at all. And while I'm at it, I'll tell him that your cook staff waters down the sauces that are mixed with the olive oil that Mr. Lacerra provides to you at a *very* reasonable price, as a courtesy to you, his friend. So it's not his oil at all that's the problem. It's your cheapskate methods of preparing your food. "

"Bullshit," the manager countered. "My staff doesn't do that."

"Bullshit on *that*! I tasted some of your watered-down sauces in the kitchen just *now*. For Christ's sake, you can tell just by looking at them. They have no heft, no texture at all." Benny hadn't actually seen or tasted anything like that, but he decided Teena Vaughn's word was good enough—and *convenient* enough—for him.

De Cresenzo just stood staring off into space as if weighing the consequences of various actions. Benny stared at him confidently, although most of the confidence was a bluff. (He knew De Cresenzo could really open a can of worms for him.)

After a quiet minute, with neither man saying a word, De Cresenzo softened. "Look, man, give me some time to think, okay? Just a couple of hours."

A noisy city bus roared past them down Kings Highway, interrupting the conversation for a moment.

"Think about *this*," Benny said. "Mr. Lacerra likes to keep his regular customers happy. So this is what I'm prepared to do. That oil you've been buying is perfectly good. But from now on, as a special favor to you, for every dozen bottles you purchase, Mr. Lacerra will add two bottles of the very finest olive oil you can get anywhere. I mean, absolute top-of-the-line stuff, imported from the old country."

The offer seemed to calm De Cresenzo down a little. But he insisted, "My chefs are great. We don't cut no corners."

"Look," Benny said. "Let's stop the pissing contest and talk like businessmen. You take the deal and improve your kitchen ethic, and I tell Mr. Lacerra everything's copacetic at Café Bari. And you get that top-of-the-line oil to boot. Nobody's bothered; everybody's content. What do you say?"

"That waitress tell you anything?" the manager wanted to know.

"She *got* something to tell me I should know about?"

"No."

Benny popped a Marlboro Light in his mouth and lit it. "Jesus, relax, will you? I wanted to get a look at her up close." He tapped De Cresenzo on the shoulder. "Don't tell me *you* haven't taken a close look."

Then he laughed. And De Cresenzo laughed with him.

"How can you not?" the manager asked. "I mean, Christ, look at her."

Benny puffed on the smoke.

"So . . . we okay now?"

"Yeah, I guess so."

"Use the top-notch oil for your best customers. You know, a special reserve for special people."

"Fine."

"Then I'll see you soon."

They shook hands.

"Ciao," they both said, almost simultaneously.

But as Benny walked away, De Cresenzo muttered "Asshole!" under his breath.

Benny didn't hear it.

The next time Benny saw Mr. Lacerra he told him he had the problem at Café Bari all straightened out.

Then he handed Mr. Lacerra an envelope.

Benny felt good about handing *this* one over.

It was the first one in a long time he was giving Lacerra knowing that Gourmet Express was back in the black financially.

He stuck a few hundred in another envelope. This was a bonus for Joey, who De Cresenzo had called "goofy."

De Cresenzo wasn't totally wrong about that.

Joey *was* a little odd. But, Benny knew, he was good people, totally trustworthy.

And Benny's best friend.

Joey deserved the money. And Benny swore to himself that if he ever became *really* successful, Joey, a little goofy or not, would always be taken care of.

Fish and Chicken

—

Baked snapper in sea-salt crust

Chicken with fresh artichokes & sausage

⟶ Baked Snapper ⟶

In a large pan, stuff fresh snapper with lemons and fresh herbs.
In a large bowl, add kosher salt and fold in egg whites.
Apply and pack salt mixture all over the snapper.
Bake until done.

⟶ Chicken with Fresh Artichokes & Sausage ⟶

Cut chicken into eighths, then flour.
Brown in sauté pan. Remove.
Clean and slice fresh artichokes; sauté, adding garlic, onions, and sausage.
Add chicken.
Add veal and chicken stock; cover and bake until tender.

Fourth Course:
Fish and Chicken

Benny checked the brand of rice that Il Bambino used. It was good enough, but not the kind he would have preferred. This stuff you had to watch like a hawk or, without warning, it would overcook and wind up all gummy, like rice from a cheap Chinese take-out place.

Benny opened the door of the oven, and the aroma of the snapper he had baking wafted out. It was mouthwatering. The snapper still had a minute or two to bake, though, so he reclosed the door.

He was preparing artichokes for the accompanying chicken dish when the dining area suddenly went quiet. Benny looked through the small window and saw two uniformed police officers standing just inside the entrance door.

"Don't let us interrupt your dinner, gentlemen," the taller cop, a sergeant, said.

Then he headed for the kitchen while his partner stayed by the door.

Benny braced himself. What the hell was *this* all about? A coincidence? Or was this arranged by . . .

The sergeant opened the door and stuck his head in the kitchen.

"Everything okay back here?" the sergeant asked.

"Yes, sir, officer . . . I mean, sergeant," Benny answered. "Everything's great."

The sergeant stepped into the kitchen, letting the door swing closed behind him. "Since when are you open on Monday nights? You're usually closed, right?"

"Usually," Benny replied. "But tonight we've got a private party going on."

He checked the sausages he had sizzling on the grill.

"I can see that," the cop said. "Somebody's birthday?"

"I'm not sure."

"Angelo around?"

"Angelo Tidona?" Benny asked, remembering the name of the owner of Il Bambino. "No, he's *still* off on Monday."

The cop smiled. "Good for him."

Benny shot a glance through the window. Some of the men were talking again. The cop by the door just stared at them intently.

"You're not the usual cook, are you?" the sergeant continued.

"No. Angelo asked me to fill in until he could get a permanent chef for any Monday nights he decides to open on."

"And what's your name?"

"Lacoco. Benny Lacoco. I'd shake your hand, sergeant, but my hands are sticky with oil and carrot juice."

"That's okay."

"Ever been to my place, Pazzo Oeuf?"

The cop looked baffled. "What a 'pozzo eff'?" he asked.

Benny smiled. "Pazzo Oeuf. Crazy egg. *My* restaurant."

"Can't say I have." The sergeant looked around. "Don't you have anyone helping you? Not even a waiter?"

Benny shook his head as he moved a pot off an open flame. "Nope. Angelo couldn't get anybody. So I gotta bust my ass. But hey, I can use the money, you know?"

There was a very strange silence for a moment. Benny couldn't read what it meant, so he decided it would be better to end the silence.

"Everything okay, sergeant?" he inquired. "Anything else I can help you with?"

After a couple of seconds, the sergeant replied, "No, I guess not. How late do you figure you'll be open?"

"Not very. I hope."

The sergeant laughed. "I hear you."

Benny saw the cop by the door laugh. Somebody at the table had said something to him. Then all the guys started laughing.

The sergeant went back into the dining area and looked at the assembled guests, nodded, and continued on to stand next to his partner. They exchanged a few words, then said good night to the men, and left.

The men remained still and silent for a minute.

Then Garguilo said, "Who the fuck forgot to lock the door? Man, *anything* can walk in."

Sapienza asked, "What the hell was that all about?"

"Probably looking for a fucking payoff," Aspromonte opined. "Or a free meal."

Abbazio called out loudly, "Hey, Benny, what did that cop want?"

Benny stepped into the dining area. "Who knows? Just asked why we were open on a Monday."

"So what did you tell him?" Double A asked.

"Told him it was a private party."

Then Ianello wanted to know, "Just what *are* we celebrating, anyway?"

Everyone just gazed at him. No one said anything.

"What?" Ianello said. "Did I say something stupid? Does anybody really *know*?"

Benny wondered if Ianello was being his usual snake self or if he really *was* totally clueless.

At any rate, he simply said, "I gotta check on the fish and finish preparing the vegetables. Be back in a minute or two with the next course."

Then he ducked back into the kitchen.

He opened the oven door and looked inside. Perfect!

The cop had distracted him and he was afraid that the snapper might have overcooked. But it hadn't, so Benny removed it from the oven and placed the baking tray on a counter.

Then Benny recalled a night not totally unlike this one.

Seafood had been on the menu that night also.

And *that* was a night he couldn't possibly forget.

Benny had finally earned a vacation.

Franzo's was doing very well, its books were balanced, all the right palms were being greased, and Uncle Tony even began taking some time off.

The guy even seemed happy, something Benny hadn't really seen since he was a little boy.

Gourmet Express was in similarly good shape. Benny had had to fire one of Joey's cousins because the kid was constantly high on weed and was being rude to their customers.

But short of that, all was well.

Benny was still fencing food for Lacerra, but that activity had grown more sporadic. Sometimes he'd have lots of product to move; at other times there was little or nothing. And he and Joey had even cut way down on the oil and wine transfusions. There was really no need to take the risk all the time anymore. They only did it when they could pick up a shipment of wine extremely cheaply . . . like when a case would "fall off" a truck. Or if one or both of them were unexpectedly strapped for cash, which they rarely were at the time.

So Benny thought he'd take a week off. He let Joey know he'd be in charge for the week. He told his uncle Tony he was finally going to take some time off, and his uncle was glad for him.

Benny figured he would start his vacation the next day, a Wednesday. He didn't plan to return to either his uncle's place or his own business until the following Tuesday.

But he figured wrong.

That next day—the Wednesday—Benny got a call around noon. It was from Joey.

"Hey, what's up?" Benny said.

"Just wanted to tell you that Lacerra was here with some other guy," Joey said. "They were looking for you."

"Did they say what they wanted?"

"Lacerra said he wanted you to do something for him."

"Did he drop off stuff?"

"No. Nothing."

Benny wondered what *this* was all about now.

"Is he gonna call me?" Benny asked. "Did he say?"

Joey answered, "He wants you to meet him at Franzo's. At one o'clock."

"That gives me a half an hour," Benny thought out loud. "Did he tell you to call me?"

"Yeah. He's still sitting in a car outside, waiting for me to give him the high sign."

"Oh, okay," Benny said. "Give it to him."

"Okay, hold on."

Benny could hear some scuffling around on the other end of the phone. Then Joey returned.

"Okay, he'll see you at your uncle's."

"Thanks."

"I wonder what he's got in mind now," Joey said.

"Something private, no doubt," Benny answered.

"Yeah."

"And probably something that's gonna interfere with my week off," Benny commented. "Although I hope I'm wrong about that."

"I hope so, too."

"You're all set, right?" he asked Joey. "You sure you can handle it all?"

"Piece of cake."

"Yeah?"

"Piece of *pound* cake!" Joey added.

Benny thought about that comment, then asked, "What does *that* mean?"

"Don't mean anything," Joey replied. "It was just a joke."

"I don't get it."

"It means the same as 'piece of cake.' You know, regular cake."

"Yeah?"

"Yeah."

"What *is* 'regular' cake?"

"I don't know . . . cake!"

Benny held the receiver away from his face for a moment. Then he raised the mouthpiece to his mouth and said, "*You* are a fucking nut, you know that?"

"Yeah," Joey said, nonchalantly. "Call me later if you need me."

"I will. Bye."

Benny hung up the phone. Joey *was* a fucking nut. But Joey was the best.

Benny put aside the travel magazine he had been reading. He had to travel to Franzo's in a hurry. Any plans for a trip would have to wait at least a couple of hours.

He arrived at Franzo's promptly. He entered through the front door, and several customers who recognized him as the chef started teasing him.

"How come you no work today?" Mr. Cioffi, a retired man of at least eighty years of age, asked in imperfect English. He ate lunch at Franzo's every Wednesday and had dinner there every Friday night.

Benny walked over to him and shook his hand. "I'm taking a few days off, Mr. C.," he said. "That's okay, isn't it?"

"No." The sweet old man teased. "The food, it's not the same."

"Is it bad?" Benny asked.

"No." The old man laughed. "It's just not the same . . . and your sauce is to die for."

A sauce to die for. Now there's an idea! Benny thought, and then said, "I've always wanted to be known for my sauce. *A sauce to die for* . . . but for now, it will be our little secret, okay?"

"I won't say a word. Just promise me you'll be cooking the next time I come by."

"You've got a deal. Enjoy your lunch."

Then he turned to Mr. Lacerra, who was sitting at a corner table with another man who Benny recognized but couldn't immediately place.

"Benny, come sit down," Lacerra said, gesturing to a seat at the table.

Benny walked up to the table.

"You don't remember me, Benny?" the other man asked.

Then it sank in. "Mr. Ranallo," he exclaimed. "I'm so sorry. I *didn't* recognize you. It's been a while."

"Yes, it has," Ranallo agreed. "Sit. Please."

Benny pulled the chair back and sat. "How's Leo? I haven't seen *him* in a while either."

"Leo's doing well. He transferred to Columbia. He's in the MBA program."

"I'll have to give him a call."

"You should. He's always studying. He could use a break."

"I will. I never really properly thanked him . . . and especially *you* . . . for helping me get started in the restaurant business." Benny then turned to Lacerra. "I owe you a lot of thanks, too, Mr. Lacerra."

Lacerra just smiled. "All I ask is that when you become an internationally known chef, you welcome me into your restaurants and cook up those special recipes."

"You'll both always be welcome," Benny assured the men.

The headwaiter came over to the table. "Good afternoon, gentlemen. You, too, Mr. Lacoco."

Benny recognized the man's "joke." He had been hearing it

since he began working at Franzo's. Benny liked Nick, the old headwaiter. His association with Franzo's went back to a time when an actual member of the Franzo family owned the place, long before his uncle Tony took over.

"Get some new material, will you?" Benny said. "Don Rickles first used that line in 1954."

Lacerra and Ranallo had already ordered. Benny told the waiter he'd just have a cup of coffee and a piece of cheesecake. In a moment the waiter placed both on the table before Benny.

"Thanks," Benny said to Nick. "I might even leave you a tip."

Nick walked away, saying, "That would be a first" loud enough so the men could hear it. He never turned around.

The trio at the table laughed.

"Guy's a regular comedian," Lacerra said.

"Yeah," Benny agreed. "The customers here love him."

Then Ranallo got down to business.

"Benny, I want you to help me out with a little favor," he said.

"Sure," he answered.

"I'm having a little private dinner at Bacala's. You know the place?"

"Over near Brooklyn College?"

"That's the place. I need a very special person to prepare a meal. It's on Friday night, after eleven o'clock."

"And you want *me* to prepare the meal."

"Yes."

"I'm honored," Benny said. "I really am."

"Word has gotten around that you're absolutely *magnifico* in the kitchen," Lacerra added.

"And, even more important, that you're a man who can be counted on to be discreet," Ranallo said.

"Thank you," Benny said. Something inside him twitched when Ranallo made his last statement, though. "Is there something in particular you'd like me to prepare? Veal, maybe?"

Ranallo shook his head. "I leave that to you. Surprise us. Make something different. Something special."

"Yeah, it's gotta be special," Lacerra agreed.

"Benny," Ranallo said gently, putting his hand flat over Benny's on the table. "This is going to be a 'retirement party' for someone."

"I'll make it *very* special then," he responded.

"Yes, yes," Ranallo said, now squeezing Benny's hand. "But I don't think you understand what I'm saying to you."

Benny looked into Ranallo's eyes. He wasn't sure what he was seeing there. His glance turned to Lacerra, who leaned forward and whispered, "Benny, *we're* retiring him."

Now Benny understood. He hoped he wasn't trembling or Ranallo would feel it in his hand.

"Can we count on you?" Ranallo asked.

Benny said without hesitation, "Yes. Of course."

"So you understand why this has to be a special meal?"

"Yes."

Ranallo sat back in his chair. Benny noticed there were tears in the man's eyes. One fell down his left cheek and hung off the side of his face.

"He is a dear friend," Ranallo said softly. "This will cause me great grief."

Lacerra put his hand on Ranallo's shoulder.

"Yet it has to be done. There's no other way. The word has already come down."

Benny wanted to know what the man had done but knew better than to ask.

"You will, of course, be protected," Ranallo said to Benny. "You'll prepare the dinner, and then we'll get you safely out of the way."

"I appreciate that," Benny replied.

"A car will be sent for you Friday night." Mr. Ranallo adjusted his tie, then added, "I will see you at Bacala's then."

Ranallo extended his hand. Benny shook it. Benny knew he was being dismissed, so he stood up and turned toward the exit.

Lacerra followed him outside.

"This really sucks when this happens," Lacerra said. "But there are things more sacred than even friendship, Benny."

Benny simply nodded.

"There's *loyalty*, know what I mean?"

"Yes, sir."

"I know you do," he said, patting Benny on the back. "I can tell you that Mr. Ranallo won't forget this, Benny. You doing this is a really good move."

As if I had a choice, Benny thought. He said nothing, however.

"See you Friday," Lacerra said. "Let me get back inside. He's really down about this whole thing."

Benny turned the corner and entered the newspaper and candy store there. He bought a pack of Marlboro Lights, lit one up outside, and just stared across the street. His guts were in an uproar. He had never thought he'd get *this* far into *this* world. But now the reality was hitting him.

He *had* to do this thing on Friday, he knew that. *That* was a given. And there was nothing he could do about it. So to get his mind off his—what? guilty conscience?—he thought about the meal he would prepare.

Then an idea hit him.

Many older—or at least old school—Italians still observed the Catholic Church's law regarding eating meat on Friday, even though the ban on meat had long since vanished. And even if all those involved in this "party" on Friday weren't part of that old school, Benny thought he couldn't miss by serving seafood.

Friday night arrived and Benny saw the Cadillac pull up outside Franzo's, where he had been informed he would be picked up. He left the restaurant, a rectangular case in hand, entered the car, and sat down.

"How's it going?" the driver asked. He was one of the men who often accompanied Lacerra.

"Okay," Benny answered.

The driver stepped on the gas and drove along Twelfth Avenue. "So you're cooking up a storm tonight, huh?"

"Yeah."

"My name's Mario, by the way. I guess we never been really introduced."

"Benny. Lacoco."

"Yeah, I know," Mario said, a cigarette dangling from his lips. "I guess you used to be afraid of me."

"Yeah," Benny smiled. "Still am."

"Well, don't be. Anybody who's a friend of Mr. Lacerra's ain't got a thing to be afraid of me about."

"Thanks. That's good to know."

"What's in the case? If you don't mind me askin'."

"Some special cooking utensils, some spices and herbs, stuff like that."

"Cool! Like a doctor making a house call." Ashes from his cigarette dropped into Mario's lap when the car went over a pothole in the street.

"Yeah. Sort of," Benny answered, closing his eyes.

The small talk died down, and Mario turned up the radio. The sound of the Rascals singing "You Better Run" filled the car. Mario's head began to bob with the music, but by the time the song was over and Cousin Brucie was announcing the call letters of the radio station, Mario had pulled the car to a halt.

"How'd you get here so fast?" Benny asked.

"It's what I do," Mario said, grinning. "And I blew a few lights."

"Thanks for the ride."

"No problem." Then, as if he were urging on a performer at a concert, he said, "Knock 'em dead."

Benny ignored the unintentional irony in the remark and got out of the car.

Bacala's was fairly empty when he entered its kitchen around 9:20 P.M. Most of the dinner crowd had left to pursue whatever they did on Friday nights. Others still lingered over drinks or desserts. Benny saw no sign of either Lacerra or Ranallo.

The chef was pretty much set to leave by ten o'clock, and he seemed more than happy to leave the rest of the cleanup detail to his assistants. He didn't seem to harbor the slightest resentment over Benny being brought in for the evening.

On the contrary, he was delighted he could leave early.

"All yours," he said to Benny as he left.

By 10:30 the place was practically devoid of all customers.

Then the two men who had recruited him and their "guest" walked in. Mr. Ranallo and the man Benny didn't know sat down at a table.

Lacerra poked his head into the kitchen, where Benny was preparing risotto and tending to the bouillabaisse stock. Benny was draining the liquid through a chinois, which caught the mashed branzino, onions, fennel, and other ingredients.

"Everything okay?" Lacerra asked.

"Yeah," Benny said. But he suddenly felt a nervous knot forming in his gut. "Just tell me when you want me to have a waiter bring you appetizers."

Lacerra informed him, "The waiters have all left. So has everyone else, in case you haven't noticed."

Benny *hadn't* noticed. He'd been so wrapped up in getting the meal ready and finding his way around Bacala's not particularly well-equipped kitchen that he hadn't seen the staff leaving.

"Oh, okay," Benny said. "So *I'll* bring out the appetizers."

"Listen, Benny," Lacerra said, stepping fully into the kitchen, making sure the door closed completely behind him. "This is killing Mr. Ranallo. Alfredo was like a brother to him. Mr. Ranallo just wants to get this over with."

"Alfredo is . . . ," Benny hesitated, searching for the appropriate choice of word. He settled on ". . . the guest?"

Lacerra nodded. "Yeah. Alfredo Brandi. You ever hear of him?"

"Can't say I have."

"Well, he was . . . ," Lacerra began to explain, then thought better of it. "Never mind. It's probably better that you don't know."

Benny simply nodded in agreement.

"Just skip to the chase. Bring out whatever you have prepared all at once. Mr. Ranallo will take care of business once the food is served and everyone begins to eat."

"I understand," Benny said.

"Once you serve the food, you can leave. Mario will be in the car, around the corner on Avenue L. He'll get you away from here."

"Thanks."

"So bring the food out as soon as you can."

"It'll be out in five to ten minutes. It's almost ready."

Lacerra left the kitchen. Benny's hands starting shaking. He first noticed it when he poured the risotto on a large flat dish. He damn near spilled the bouillabaisse as he coated the rice with the hot liquid. And it got worse while he was slicing a lemon into thin slices to arrange on the plate. He damn near cut his thumb off.

Benny tried to stay focused and calm. But everything that happened next seemed to be as if seen through a cheese cloth.

He brought out a number of different dishes and arranged them on the table. He said hello to Mr. Ranallo. He saw Lacerra sitting next to a man who Benny guessed was in his fifties. He shook the man's hand and someone introduced him to Brandi. Then he asked Mr. Ranallo if they needed anything else. Ranallo said, "No, thank you." So Benny went back into the kitchen, packed up his gear, and left the restaurant.

As he headed for his ride, he half-expected to hear gunshots go off. But he heard nothing. Only his own heart beating loudly.

He got into the backseat of the car. In a couple of seconds, Mario pulled out of the parking spot and headed away.

In what seemed like an amazingly short time, Benny was home.

He got into bed, feeling slightly nauseous, wondering if he'd ever be able to sleep. But, on the contrary, within five minutes he was out cold.

The ringing phone awoke Benny the next morning. It was only a few minutes after nine o'clock.

"Hello?" Benny said, still half-asleep.

"Benny," the voice on the other end said.

He recognized the voice as Lacerra's.

"Hi," Benny said, waking up instantly. Lacerra had never called him at home before.

"Gotta talk to you. Right away."

"Okay."

"Pick you up in ten minutes."

"I'll be ready."

Benny hung up the phone and found a clean shirt to put on. Oh shit, he thought. Something went wrong. He finished getting dressed and quickly combed his hair and brushed his teeth.

As he spit the toothpaste out into the sink, he heard a car horn honking. He wiped his mouth, grabbed a jacket, and stepped outside. The same car that had driven him to Bacala's last night was idling by the curb. He noticed Lacerra in the backseat and Mario once again behind the wheel.

He opened the door and sat in the back next to Lacerra. The older man noticed the panicky look on Benny's face.

"I wake you up?" Lacerra asked.

"Yeah," Benny answered. "I guess." Then he screwed up the nerve to ask, "Is anything wrong?"

"Just that I ain't slept a wink yet," Lacerra answered. "Neither has Mario."

Benny stared at Lacerra, hoping that he'd continue his answer. He did . . . in a way.

"This is for you," he said, handing Benny a large manila envelope.

Benny took it, just staring at it.

"You gonna open it or what?" Lacerra asked.

Benny opened it. Inside was a stack of one-hundred-dollar bills tied together with a rubber band. He didn't count it.

"There must be five thousand here," Benny exclaimed.

"For a job above and beyond the call of duty." Lacerra poked Mario in the back. "Let's go to McDonald's. I'm in the mood for one of those McMuffin things."

Then he turned to Benny. "You eat that stuff, Benny? Or will I be insulting your sense of food, I guess you'd call it?"

"No," Benny uttered. "But I could use a cup of coffee."

"Good. Let's go."

As the car moved, Lacerra said, "Benny, Mr. Ranallo was *very* happy last night."

"He was?"

"Yeah, you know, other than the fact that Brandi had to go. But you made it easy for Mr. Ranallo, and he's very pleased with you."

"Then there was no trouble?" Benny asked. "Nothing went wrong? When I got your call a few minutes ago, I thought maybe I had screwed up or something."

"Screwed up? Not at all." Lacerra put his hand on Benny's shoulder. "Man, you made it all happen *naturally*."

"*I* did?"

"Yeah," Lacerra said. Then, as the car approached the fast-food joint, Lacerra leaned forward to Mario and said, "Go through the drive-through. Get me an Egg McMuffin with ham and a black coffee and get Benny . . ."

"Just a regular coffee," Benny interrupted.

". . . you heard the man."

Mario placed the order, then pulled up a few feet to the windows to pay for and get the food and coffee. At Lacerra's request, he then simply pulled into a parking spot in the McDonald's lot. Mario handed back the sandwich and two cups of coffee.

"Didn't you want anything?" Lacerra asked Mario.

"Nah," the driver answered. "My stomach feels like shit. Been smoking too much, I think."

Lacerra folded back the paper around the McMuffin and took a bite.

Benny asked, "If you don't mind me asking, what do you mean *I* made last night go naturally?"

Lacerra swallowed the mouthful of food, then drank down a bit of black coffee.

"Benny, Brandi and Mr. Ranallo used to be *really* close. As close as two guys can get, without getting all homo about it, you know? Well, Mr. Ranallo felt honor-bound to do the deed himself last night. He felt *he'd* have to retire Brandi."

"So that's what he did?"

"No," Lacerra corrected. "No. That's what *you* did."

Benny was still confused, and his face reflected his confusion.

"You did it for him, Benny. You fed Brandi that risotto. You made it in fish stock or something, right? "

"Yeah, bouillabaisse," Benny said. "But I still don't get it."

"Brandi was allergic to seafood. And I mean *big-time* allergic. I guess the old guy wasn't paying attention. So he wolfed down that risotto stuff you made. Then he started—I swear to fucking God—to turn blue and he started wheezing and choking and pulling at his shirt collar. The fucking guy was half dead before Ranallo and I helped speed up the process."

Benny still looked confused.

"It took a minute or two before Mr. Ranallo realized—or *re-*

membered maybe, I don't know which—that Brandi was allergic, but once he did, all we had to do was sit back and watch."

Benny tried not to display any emotion whatsoever. He simply listened.

"It wasn't pretty, I can tell you that, but at least Mr. Ranallo didn't have to see bits of his friend's brains splattered all around, you know? And I gotta tell you, it was all over pretty quick."

Then everyone in the car remained silent for a moment, perhaps out of respect for the deceased.

Lacerra put his arm around Benny and continued, "So you see, you made it easy. No blood, no mess, no nothing, except for food and the mess all over the floor when Brandi fell out of his chair and dragged half the table with him. And the beautiful thing—and the thing that Mr. Ranallo is most happy about—is that it all seemed natural. It was an *accident*, understand? Brandi did it himself."

Then Lacerra added, "Well, mostly. Anyhow, everything's cool now. It seemed like an accident. Mr. Ranallo's *so* pleased, at least as much as can be expected given the loss of his friend."

Benny was speechless.

"So, here's to you," Lacerra said, raising his cup of McDonald's coffee to Benny. Then he took a sip.

Benny raised his cup too and took a swallow.

"Mr. Ranallo told me to tell you that he's gonna take care of you, Benny. You've made a real friend in him. You'll see. And one thing I can tell you about Mr. Ranallo is that he always takes care of his friends."

Benny smiled and managed to keep the smile even while he remembered that Mr. Brandi was also Mr. Ranallo's friend.

"He also wants you to take these," Lacerra said.

He handed Benny two Delta airline tickets.

"A few days in Vegas at the MGM Grand. Have a ball. Go see Sinatra and Dino. Or that Lola Falana if you like the dark meat, you know what I mean? You leave tonight, so go get ready."

"Is this for me to hide out for a while?" Benny asked.

Lacerra laughed. "You got no reason to hide. Don't worry about anything. You got nothing to worry about. Absolutely nothing. Just go and have a good time."

"Thanks, Mr. Lacerra," Benny said.

Then the conversation drifted off, and Benny was dropped off back at his house.

When he sat down in his kitchen, he placed the envelope full of money on the table.

Now, he realized, he *really* needed that vacation. Because he figured that when he returned, his "minor league" status might be over.

He might have just been promoted into the big leagues . . . big leagues with big friends—and maybe really big obligations.

Pasta

—

Perciatelli
with sardines, fennel greens, toasted bread crumbs

Rigatoni
with shiitake mushrooms, smoked mozzarella, & arugula

Orecchiette
with sausage & broccoli rabe pesto

‐ Perciatelli ‐

Sauté garlic and onions until soft.
Add sardines, white wine, clam juice, two cups of water, saffron,
tomato paste, raisins, and pine nuts.
Cook perciatelli in salted water.
Add fennel tops; drain.
Toss pasta with sauce.
Top with toasted bread crumbs.

‐ Rigatoni ‐

Sauté shiitake mushrooms, garlic, and onions until soft.
Add veal stock.
Cook rigatoni in salted water; drain.
Toss pasta with mushroom sauce, arugula, and diced smoked mozzarella.
Serve.

‐ Orecchiette ‐

Blanch broccoli rabe.
Sauté garlic, red pepper flakes, olive oil.
Puree broccoli rabe and garlic mixture in robot coupe,
salt and pepper to taste.
Cook orecchiette in salted water, drain.
Grill and slice sausage.
Toss with pureed sauce; top with sausage.

— Fifth Course: Pasta —

"Hey, Benny, ya rat bastard!" Palumbo called out loudly. "Come here, will ya?"

Benny recognized Pally's voice and thought about opening the door, taking the paring knife he was holding, and throwing it at him instead of answering him. With any luck he'd hit him square in the throat, severing his thoroughly annoying and unceasingly used vocal chords.

Instead, he calmed himself, put the utensil down, and stepped into the dining area.

"What can I do for you now?" Benny asked sarcastically.

"Some of us got a bet going," Pally said.

"And?"

"And we wanna know whose dick you hadda suck to open that restaurant of yours."

Benny noticed the look on Double A's face. His friend seemed nervous, knowing enough about his friend to know that Benny's reaction to Pally was *never* predictable.

Benny wiped his hands on a small white towel, and without making any eye contact with Pally at all, answered, "Your mother's."

Pally's reaction *was* predictable. As usual, he could dish it out but couldn't take it. He shot up out of his chair and screamed, "You motherfucker! Who the fuck do you think you're fuckin' talkin' to?"

Ischia and Di Pietro held the riled Palumbo by the arms so he couldn't move away from the table.

"Calm down," Ischia said. "For Christ's sake."

"Fuck you, too," Pally said.

Double A said, "Man, it's just a damn joke."

"Joke, my ass," Pally said. "Nobody talks about my mother like that."

"Then don't ask stupid questions," Benny commented coolly. "Especially if you don't want answers."

Di Pietro forced Pally back into his chair. "Sit the fuck down, will ya?"

"Yeah," Ianello added. "We're not here to fight among ourselves."

"And you gotta be crazy," Sapienza said, "to bust the balls of the guy who's cooking your meal. I mean, jeez!"

Pally, still steaming under the collar, checked out the gaze of several of his compatriots. From their faces and their comments he knew he would have little or no support from them if he continued his attacks on Benny.

So he shook off Di Pietro's grasp. "Let me the fuck go."

Di Pietro raised his hands in front of him in a gesture that said "whatever."

"Here, have some vino," Aspromonte said, pouring the liquid into Pally's glass. "Calm down."

Benny reentered the kitchen without saying another word. But he couldn't help *thinking* how much he hoped that if anyone *was* getting popped tonight, it was Palumbo.

Benny calmly checked the pasta dishes. Three separate dishes stood on the counter before him. The perciatelli with sardines and fennel greens only needed one more ingredient. So Benny coated the dish with toasted bread crumbs.

Then he turned to the rigatoni. The shiitake mushrooms and chunks of smoked mozzarella had already been added to the pasta. Benny added the arugula and stood back and visually admired his work.

He could hear the men talking, but, except for a word here and a phrase there, couldn't actually make out the gist of the discussion.

Then the door opened.

In walked Palumbo.

Alone.

He just stared at Benny, standing still and tall with his hands by his sides.

Benny turned toward him. Pally looked like some urban version of a western gunfighter about to "draw."

"Yeah?" Benny asked, trying to appear disinterested. "What?"

Pally raised his left hand to rub his cheek. "I came in to call a truce. The guys think we should call a truce."

"That so?" Benny asked. "You sure you just ain't afraid I'll spill some Clorox or something into your food?"

Pally was going to respond with an insult about how all Benny's meals tasted like Clorox, but thought better of it.

"C'mon," he said. "We gonna call a truce or not?"

Benny knew that Pally was only doing this because the rest of the guys had gotten on his case, but he went along with it anyway, even though he had no faith in this truce ever extending beyond this night. And maybe not even *that* long.

"Yeah, sure," Benny finally answered, extending his arms.

Palumbo stepped up to him, and the two men embraced silently for a few seconds.

Then Palumbo returned to the dining area. Benny heard the rest of the guys break into applause.

He also heard Di Pietro say, "Now they can be lovers again. Here, everybody have some more wine."

Benny gave the orecchiette with sausage and broccoli rabe pesto a slight toss in the bowl. Everything for the next course was ready now. Before him on the counter lay a veritable orgy of pasta dishes. They were dishes that Benny himself thoroughly enjoyed preparing—and eating. He often made these at home for his wife and children, though his son simply refused to eat sardines, no matter how his father tried to persuade and cajole him to try them.

He hoped the guys would appreciate not just the taste of the meals but the creativity that went into them. Not to mention how great they *looked*.

But he figured he was hoping for too much there. He'd settle for just hearing the word *deliciosa*.

Benny poured himself a glass of pinot grigio from a bottle he had brought with him to the kitchen. He breathed in its bouquet, thinking it was pretty good stuff, not the usual middle-grade stuff most restaurants had.

And as he savored the taste of the wine and started bringing in the three pasta dishes he had prepared, he thought about how he had helped a friend, one who had had to unload his vast stock of wine quickly.

One thing you could say for Mr. Ranallo was that he always kept his word. And, of course, it never hurt when a higher-up was the father of one of your friends.

Since his return from his almost-all-expenses paid trip to Vegas—a trip to the desert gambling capital from which Benny actually returned with seventeen thousand dollars *more* than when he had left—Benny's life began to change.

He moved out of his parents' house and found a fairly spacious apartment in a well-maintained building on Shore Road. The view from his windows overlooked the Narrows; at night the spectacle of the ocean, its bobbing waters lit up here and there with reflections of the lights on the Verrazano Bridge and an occasional passing ship, always brought a certain comfort to him.

He bought himself a sporty navy blue Honda, fully loaded. It wasn't a Maserati, but then again he didn't want to risk driving—or parking—a car of *that* class on the streets of Brooklyn. Or even in the basement garage of his apartment house.

He wasn't ready for that class of car yet, and the Honda was fine for now.

But the best new part of Benny's life was Pazzo Oeuf. Mr. Ranallo gave Benny the freedom to name the restaurant himself, and he chose Pazzo Oeuf for many reasons. Benny thought it was a catchy name and said a lot about the range of the dishes, the variety of the meal offerings, and the ambience he hoped the place would have. And the choice of a half-Italian, half-French name was purely intentional.

Benny often had to pinch himself to make sure he wasn't dreaming or hallucinating the whole thing. He was only in his mid-twenties, and he was the chef in his *own* restaurant! Benny knew that Mr. Ranallo had set up the whole thing, but he still couldn't believe it. Yet all the papers—the real estate documents, the licenses, just about everything—had Benny's name on them.

He never really asked *how* Mr. Ranallo had managed all this so quickly. There were some things you *just* didn't ask, he knew. But within two months of Benny's return from Vegas, Pazzo Oeuf was his, fully equipped with the finest stoves, ovens, cookwear, everything that could be purchased. All he had to do was hire his own staff.

And he set out to do that right away.

First, though, there were some matters to take care of.

When he told his uncle Tony, his uncle already knew. That was no surprise to Benny. Uncle Tony wished him well and asked him to *please* still come by Franzo's once in a while to see how the staff was doing. Benny assured him he would.

Benny took Joey Arso out for drinks at Pip's, a popular saloon/comedy club in Sheepshead Bay that had seen better days but still featured a promising up-and-coming comedian every once in a while. On the night they went, the comedy act was a jerk with a ventriloquist's dummy. Joey laughed a lot at the guy, so Benny didn't mind suffering through the guy's pathetic routine. Joey's cackling made Benny laugh, so it all seemed to balance out.

When the unfunny comedian's tortured act ended, he asked Joey if he wanted to come into Pazzo Oeuf with him or take over Gourmet Express. Joey's answer didn't surprise him.

"Hey, Benny," Joey said. "It's not like I don't appreciate your thinking of me when it comes to the Express. But I'm getting tired of it. I'd rather come into the restaurant with you."

"You sure?" Benny asked.

"Yeah. If you got a place for me. You know, something to do."

"What do you *want* to do?" Benny asked.

"I don't know," Joey said, shrugging his shoulders. "It's not like I can cook or anything. I wouldn't even be a good waiter. You know me. I'd spill ziti all over everyone."

"You put yourself down too much, man," Benny told him.

"But what *would* I do? I don't want to be just a . . . a load . . . just sorta hanging around."

Benny laughed. "You were just a load when Gourmet Express started, weren't you?"

Joey laughed too. "Hey, screw you, man. You couldn't have done shit with that business if it wasn't for me helping your ass out."

"That's true. That's why I want you in with this, too. It won't be much different. I'll still be the commander of the kitchen, and you'll still be my first mate."

"But what'll I do?"

Benny sat back in his chair. "Stop asking me that. It all fell into place before. It'll happen again."

"You sure?"

"Sure."

"Okay, then."

The two sealed the deal with a handshake.

"But I *still* don't know . . ."

Benny slammed down his drink. "If you say that again, I'm gonna break your fucking hands."

Joey acted startled. But then he said, "Don't do that. I won't be able to jerk off."

"And then you'll have no sex life at all."

"Hey, screw you!"

"Fuck off! Let's get out of here before that dumb-ass ventriloquist comes back on."

"Right."

The men left Sheepshead Bay and headed home.

Benny's possession of the newly named Pazzo Oeuf was to begin in two weeks. By the end of the first week, his whole staff was pretty much hired, mostly friends he had made traveling in the restaurant circle, friends who were extremely good at what they did, be it in the kitchen or the dining room. He hired a couple of neighborhood kids he knew to serve as busboys. After seven or eight days, he had just about everyone he needed.

Except for one person he wanted.

So he drove to Café Bari one night about ten o'clock and parked across the street. The lights were still on in the place, but there didn't seem to be any customers inside. Benny noticed some of the staff moving around the place, cleaning up.

Then *she* left through the front door.

Teena Vaughn was wearing a tan suede jacket with fur around the collar. She headed down the street by herself, pulling the jacket closer to her to protect her from the chilly autumn air.

Benny got out of his car, quickly walked down the other side of the street, crossed at the corner, and when he was a few feet behind her, called out Teena's name.

The young woman turned, startled.

"Do you remember me?" Benny asked, keeping his distance. "I didn't mean to scare you."

It took her a minute to recognize him.

"Yes, sure," she said. "Mr. Lacoco, right? You inspected the restaurant a while ago."

"God," Benny exclaimed. "I'm flattered you remembered my name."

Teena seemed suddenly nervous. "Yeah, well . . . what can I do for you?"

Benny tried hard not to act like some nervous schoolboy, but he wasn't sure he was pulling it off. "I was wondering," he said, "if I could offer you a job."

"Huh?" she uttered, confused.

"I'll be opening a new restaurant next week. Actually, I'll be assuming ownership."

She just stared at him, not comprehending.

"I was hoping I could steal you away from Café Bari."

Teena looked off across the street as if she were trying to make sense of it all. "You want me to come work for you?"

"Yes," Benny answered.

Then she suddenly smiled. "Really?"

"Really."

Her smile just as suddenly turned to a frown. "Why?" she asked in a foreboding tone.

Benny couldn't find an appropriate answer to vocalize. He thought of *many* answers, all of which were true: she was fantastic looking; she was sexy as hell; she was someone he *definitely* wanted to know better; and she seemed to know her way around a restaurant. But he said none of those things.

Instead, he said, "Listen, could I buy you a drink or something? It's cold out here."

She seemed taken aback and fidgeted on her feet.

Benny noticed she was uncomfortable. "I'm not trying to hit on you. I swear this is a legitimate job offer."

She stood her ground and answered, "Yeah, well, I've heard that before."

"You've had other job offers?"

"I've had *all kinds* of offers."

Then there was a moment of quiet, except for the traffic passing them in the night. Benny felt like it was some sort of stalemate. But he didn't want to blow this by being pushy or coming on too eagerly.

"Okay, look," he said. "I'm sorry I approached you this way. I probably should have done this during the day and not out in the street. If I give you my phone number, will you call me tomorrow and we can discuss the job then? I won't ask for your number."

She said she'd take his number.

She *didn't* say she'd call.

Benny cursed himself for not having a business card. All he had was an old Gourmet Express card. So he flipped it over and wrote down the number of Pazzo Oeuf.

"I'm in and out all day, but you can reach me at this number," he said, handing her the card.

She took it, looked at the front and the back, and shoved it into her handbag. "Thanks," she said.

Benny waved his arms in frustration, then caught himself doing it, and quickly stopped. Yep, he thought to himself, I'm acting like a high school kid asking a girl to the junior prom.

"I'm sorry," he repeated. "But think about calling. I could *really* use a talented hostess."

"Oh, a hostess, huh?" she mocked. "De Cresenzo said I'd be a hostess too. But in all the time I've been here, all I've ever done is wait tables and try not to spill the food and drinks on the customers. So I've heard that 'hostess' line before."

Benny sighed in exasperation. "Look, I don't know what De Cresenzo told you or even if he *knows* the difference between a waitress and a hostess. But *I* do. If I wanted you for a waitress, I would have said so. I need a *hostess*. Okay?"

"Okay."

Then he said good night and walked back across the street toward his car. Well, fucked that up, he thought. Nice fucking going.

But Teena called out to him before he hit the pavement on the other side of the street. "Hey! You know what?"

Benny turned, surprised she was talking to him. "What?" he asked.

She crossed her arms against her chest, pocketbook dangling in front of her. "I *could* use a cup of coffee. There's a diner on the next block."

Benny smiled and returned to her side of the street.

"My pleasure," he stated. And they headed for the diner, walking side by side.

The rest of that encounter went extremely well. Over coffee and huge slices of blueberry pie, Benny persuaded Teena to work at his restaurant. She would start in ten days and be paid 50 percent more than she was making at Café Bari. There was a little more negotiating that went on, particularly concerning nights off, which, she told Benny, might come with little warning. She was determined to make it in show business, she told him, and particularly had her eye on becoming a Radio City Rockette.

Benny was amenable to most of her requests.

He didn't care about the small stuff; he just wanted her around him.

When the discussion was over, Benny offered to drive her home.

But, no surprise to him, she turned him down, saying she didn't live far away from the diner and she walked home at night all the time.

"Besides," she said, "I'm armed." She showed him the can of mace she had in her purse.

Why she showed it to him, Benny wasn't quite sure. Was it to reassure him that she'd be alright? Or was it a message to him that *he* better not cross any boundaries? He took it, actually, as both.

But as he drove home, he had a good feeling about Teena. After all, she *did* have that coffee with him and she *did* accept the job.

And—most of all—he would have her around him.

A lot.

He knew he probably could have been more forceful, more aggressive, with her. But she was like a beautiful, delicate porcelain figure, and he didn't want to be the proverbial bull in the china shop.

She was worth having, he assessed. And therefore she was worth waiting for.

When her first day came, she arrived early, dressed in tight black silky slacks and a denim blouse. Benny had trouble keeping his eyes off her. Her blouse was not particularly revealing—although a couple of inches of cleavage was visible—and her slacks clung to her long, muscular yet feminine legs and ass like a second skin.

She worked herself into the swing of things easily and beautifully.

She memorized the specials, three of Benny's original culinary creations, and didn't hesitate to ask him whatever she didn't know regarding ingredients, preparation, whatever. She was patient with the customers, courteous to the other staff, and more than efficient in every way.

Benny was *thrilled* with her. Besides looking great—Benny

couldn't stop gazing at her shapely dancer's legs—he was delighted with her professional ability. He had, without question, picked a winner. Whatever else happened between them would make any relationship they had that much better.

But Benny knew he'd better slow down and take his time. It would all be worth it in the end. It was worth it *already*.

The opening of Pazzo Oeuf was a huge success.

The place was packed with friends and curious neighborhood folks with a culinary sense; a great deal of free wine flowed throughout the place; and the local newspaper, *The Ridge Reporter*, sent a writer and photographer to cover the opening. Several photos of "Chef Benny Lacoco," as the story referred to him, were taken. Benny liked the attention, but he made sure that he got Teena in most of the photos too.

A little cheesecake never hurt, he knew.

And then it just took off.

Business was great. And it kept getting better.

Many of Benny's friends were coming around. Those in the know told him he was a "made man."

The New York daily tabloids reviewed Pazzo Oeuf. Both the *New York Daily News* and the *New York Post* gave Benny's place favorable ratings; the restaurant critic in the *News* even called Benny "a brilliant innovator" in the kitchen. *The New York Times* hadn't even mentioned Pazzo Oeuf in its pages, but Benny half-expected that. He knew it took something big to get those critics to visit the outer boroughs.

Benny started spending money. His wardrobe improved; his Visa card statements revealed purchases from Bloomingdale's and

Lord and Taylor where once they showed more charges at Macy's or the Gap. He bought himself a state-of-the-art television, videotape recorder, and stereo. He wasn't spending like a lunatic, but now that he was making some real money, he made a conscious effort to live the life he could now afford to live.

And, of course, he always sent Mr. Ranallo his cut of the profits. Ranallo had never really been specific about what his cut would be, but Benny sent him what he thought was a generous portion of the profits, and he never heard a word of complaint from Ranallo or his associates.

Strangely, he hadn't seen or heard from Mr. Lacerra for months. Benny sometimes wondered what was happening with him. After all, he owed Lacerra quite a lot too.

Then one night he found out. From Mr. Lacerra himself.

Benny's crew had all left the restaurant late on a Saturday night. The place had been packed since lunch time. Benny was exhausted. He sat at a table drinking a Drambuie on the rocks with a twist of lemon. Drinking after closing time wasn't something he usually did, nor was this his usual drink. But he just felt like sitting in his restaurant—feeling good—so he did. All alone. It would only take him a few minutes to get home, he thought, so why the hell not?

He thought about Teena. They seemed to be getting friendlier, and, at times, he thought, she was *obviously* flirting with him. And then there were the times she would watch him work in the kitchen. Often, it seemed to Benny, she watched him with . . . admiration. A couple of times she had even allowed him to drive her home.

But Benny was still hesitant. He didn't want to move too soon. But he knew that the day was coming closer when he'd flat out ask her out. That day, he knew, would be soon. He could feel it. He thought she might be feeling it too.

His thoughts of Teena were suddenly interrupted by someone knocking on one of the windows of the restaurant. Benny pretended not to notice at first, ignoring whoever it was entirely. But when the knocking persisted and got louder, Benny knew he had better have words with this pain in the ass—whoever he was—before he broke the goddamned window.

Benny unlocked the front door and stepped outside. A man, hunched over, his jacket collar drawn up around his neck, stepped closer to him.

"We're closed," Benny said. "It's one in the morning."

The man turned his face up to Benny. It was Lacerra.

And he looked like death warmed over.

"Benny," he said, "can we talk somewhere?"

Startled, Benny answered, "Yeah, sure. Come on in."

Both entered the restaurant, but before either man sat down, Lacerra asked, "Look, can we cut the lights? Or go in the back?"

Benny was about to ask why but didn't. It was clear *something* was wrong, so he shut the lights.

Lacerra pulled out a chair from under a table away from the door or any window.

"Want a drink?" Benny asked.

"No, thanks," Lacerra said.

Benny brought what was left of his Drambuie to the table. He sat down opposite Lacerra.

"Benny, I need help," Lacerra said. "I'm fucked."

"Fucked how?" Benny asked, honest concern in his voice.

"You haven't heard anything?"

"Heard what?"

"Anything. About me."

"No. I've been busy with this place. I haven't been socializing much."

Lacerra looked like he was about to cry. "Please, Benny. Don't bullshit me. If you want me to get the fuck out, I will. Only *please* don't bullshit me."

"I'm not bullshitting you."

Lacerra rubbed the sides of his face with the open palms of his hands. "Okay."

"What the hell is going on?" Benny asked. "I was just thinking the other day that I hadn't seen you in quite a while."

"Yeah, well . . . have you seen Ranallo recently?"

"Saw him about a week and a half ago. He came in here with a couple of guys I didn't know."

"He didn't say nothing? Nothing about me?"

"No. Nothing."

Lacerra sat back in the chair. "I'm fucked, Benny. I'm in the deepest shit I've ever been in."

"How?" Benny asked, then realized the question was badly phrased. "I mean, what happened?"

Lacerra looked away from him. "I'll spare you all the details, Benny. Let's just say that if I don't come up with roughly a quarter of a million real soon, I'm a fuckin' dead man. Some shit I was into went bad."

"I can lend you some money," Benny offered. "But I don't have that kind of cash."

Lacerra's face almost broke into a smile. Almost.

"I know you don't," he continued. "But I appreciate the offer anyway."

"So what do you want me to do?"

"Benny, I hate to do this, but I gotta call in any favors you owe me. And I think you know you owe me some."

"You *and* Mr. Ranallo," Benny agreed.

Lacerra sat up straight and squinted, as if someone had just shoved a pole up his ass. "Ranallo's the man putting the squeeze on me. So it might be a good idea from now on not to mention the two of us in the same breath."

Benny finished off the last of the Drambuie. "You sure you don't want a drink?"

Lacerra shook his head. "I'm gonna make this short and sweet because my just sitting here with you could get you screwed too. I only got one way out of this fix, Benny, and you're the only guy I can trust to help me get out of it. At least, I think I can trust you."

Benny heard Lacerra's last statement as a prompt for him to say "yes," so he did.

"Ranallo's catching heat from the big guys about the money, so naturally the shit's trickled down to me. I owe a fuckin' *ton* of money. And I only got one way to get it."

"How's that?" Benny asked.

"Wine."

"I don't get it."

"Switching stuff. Taking okay wine and relabeling it as expensive imported stuff."

Benny suddenly got nervous. "You want me to help you do that?"

Lacerra sat forward. "Look, Benny, I know you used to pull that old switcheroo at your delivery place."

Benny said nothing. He didn't think Lacerra had known anything about the "transfusions" that went on at Gourmet Express.

"I thought it was clever," Lacerra went on. "And I wasn't about to hit you up for a piece of *everything*, you know. I figured, hey, let the kid make a few bucks."

Unwittingly, Benny exclaimed, "Shit!"

"Ranallo knew too. He didn't give a shit, either."

"Really?"

"Yeah," Lacerra said. "Let me tell you something. There's almost nothing you can do that somebody in this organization doesn't know something about. I fuckin' forgot that for a while. That's why I'm gonna get it up the ass if I don't square myself real soon. And that's why I'm asking for your help."

Benny realized he was between the proverbial rock and a hard place. "So you're asking me to get involved in something that pits me against Mr. Ranallo?"

Lacerra looked down at the top of the table. "Yeah, in a way. It sucks, doesn't it? But I'm telling you, I got no one else to turn to. Right now, I'm a fucking outcast. Anyhow, Ranallo doesn't have to know you helped me."

Benny sat forward in his seat. "Didn't you just tell me that there's no hiding anything?"

"Yeah," Lacerra said. "I did say that. I don't know what the fuck I'm talking about anymore."

Then there were a couple of minutes of absolute quiet. Lacerra looked like he was about to cry.

Benny *did* feel a sense of obligation to Lacerra, but he really didn't want to get involved in this without knowing the full story. So he asked another question, which he hoped would help clarify the whole situation.

"What exactly do you want me to do? Switch some wine around and fence it?"

"That would be the second part of it," Lacerra answered.

"What's the first part?"

"I own a winery out on the island. With one of my cousins."

Benny said, "Then that should make it a little easier. But to get two hundred and fifty G's, you better have a lot of stock."

"I know. This was a good year. There's a lot of wine. But you're right: it ain't gonna get me *that* much money."

Benny could sense that there was more information coming. He was right.

"That's why after the stock is out of the place, *it has to be torched.*"

Benny heard the words, but they didn't sink in immediately. It took another thirty seconds before they finally did.

"It has to be torched."

"You're gonna torch the place?" Benny asked. He just wanted to make sure he had it straight.

"I have to," Lacerra said. "That insurance money is my only way out. That and whatever wine I can move."

"You want *me* to torch it?" Benny hoped Lacerra would answer in the negative.

"Not necessarily," Lacerra said. "I can get guys to do that. My cousin's got a couple of friends who can take care of that. What I'd need you to do is get as much wine out of there as you can *before* the place goes up in flames. Then move it for me. Repackaged, like. You know, like you used to do."

Benny picked up on Lacerra's not very subtle reminder that he knew about Benny's previous wine "transfusions." He realized that if he helped Lacerra, it might land him in an even deeper pile of shit than the one Lacerra was in. On the other hand, he could say no and tell Lacerra to find someone else. He could even tell

Mr. Ranallo that Lacerra had come to him. Ranallo would appreciate that, and *that* could pay off for Benny. But if Lacerra burned down his winery anyway and got whatever insurance money he hoped for, and then cleared himself with Ranallo and the other higher-ups, Benny would catch endless hell from Lacerra.

It was a tough call. Tougher than any football pick he had ever had to make.

He decided to aid Lacerra.

Benny *did* owe the man something. Yes, he'd help him. Within reason.

Benny agreed to move the wine for him. He said he'd enlist Joey and a few other guys to go out to the North Fork with containers and trucks and whatever else they needed. Then the wine could be stored and repackaged at different locations. Some of it could be stored in Pazzo Oeuf's basement. Some of it at his apartment. Some at Joey's place. And Lacerra would have to come up with some other spots too.

So Benny agreed. But he told Lacerra he wanted nothing to do with the actual torching of the place. None of his guys would be involved with that at all.

Lacerra shook his hand. "Benny, I appreciate this. I always knew you were a right guy. I *always* knew that."

"When do you want the stuff moved?" Benny asked.

"As soon as possible."

"Call me here tomorrow night," Benny said. "I have to get in touch with some people. See when they're available, what kind of trucks I can get. I should know something tomorrow night."

"I will, Benny. This time of night alright?"

"Yeah. Call me here around midnight."

The two men stood up, shook hands, and Lacerra headed for

the door. "Thanks, Benny. I'll never ask for another favor—*ever*—if you do this for me. *Ever!*"

Benny nodded. "Talk to you tomorrow."

Lacerra disappeared into the night. Benny put on his jacket and looked around Pazzo Oeuf one last time. Then he too left the place, locking it up.

He moved down the sidewalk to where his car was parked. He almost tripped over a cracked piece of sidewalk. And, strangely, an old rhyme came back to him:

Step on a crack
Break your mother's back

It was a stupid old game and rhyme that kids used to play. You had to avoid stepping on any seams in the pavement on your block or you lost the game.

Benny knew he would soon be playing a new game by helping Lacerra. Only this was no kid's game. And it wasn't his mother's back he was worried about.

It was *his*.

When Pazzo Oeuf opened late the next morning for lunch, Benny pulled Joey downstairs where they could talk and not be overheard. He explained what had happened the night before and that he had promised Lacerra that he'd help him. He also told him that he couldn't do that unless Joey was involved too.

Joey didn't hesitate to volunteer. He was more than willing to drive a truck out to Long Island and do whatever else he had to do. He told Benny he'd been bored lately and could use the adventure, as he put it. And when Benny said he'd need a few more guys to help move the wine, Joey, not surprisingly, said he could get a few relatives to help.

That night, Benny heard from Lacerra again. He called precisely at midnight. They coordinated days and times that trucks could go to the North Fork winery and move out the stock of wine. It was decided that it should be done in shifts, not all at once, to avoid suspicion. Some of the trucks would be provided by Lacerra himself, and Joey and company would use them. Others would be rentals: a U-Haul truck, a Ryder van, whatever. They would move as much of the wine as they could in the next five days.

Lacerra told him that the fire would happen the following weekend.

Benny reminded Lacerra that he didn't want to be involved in *that* in *any* way.

In the days that followed Benny tried to keep his mind on the restaurant, but it was difficult.

Joey was traveling out to Long Island every day and bringing wine to various places in Brooklyn in containers of assorted sizes. Benny himself took an evening and the following afternoon off to help. He drove a Budget rental truck to the winery and helped load container after container of Chardonnay and varietal wines.

By Friday afternoon the back room of Gourmet Express— which Benny still owned, though Joey's relatives did most of the day-to-day work—was filled with bottles and small vats of wine. More were stashed in the basement of Pazzo Oeuf, some was kept in Joey's apartment and in the garages of his parents and cousins, and a good deal took up a lot of space in Benny's Shore Road apartment. Hundreds of empty bottles were taken from the winery, and they were stashed wherever Benny could find room.

Lacerra called Benny late Friday night at the restaurant, but the place was still pretty full of customers, so Benny said he'd call him back. He returned the call about an hour and a quarter later.

Lacerra asked if they could make one more haul on Saturday morning. But Benny had had enough for many reasons, though he only mentioned a couple to Lacerra.

"To be honest," he told Lacerra, actually *being* partially honest, "I got nowhere else to put the stuff. Or the bottles. So unless you know some place, I don't think I can manage another haul. Also, my guys are rattled. They've been busting their balls all week and I've been promising them a piece of the action, but since I don't know exactly what that is, I've been kinda vague about it."

"Okay," Lacerra said. "I guess we got all we can get. And give your guys whatever you feel is cool, Benny. You'll get it all back from me—their money, the rentals, everything—as soon as I collect from the insurance company. You know I'm good for the money."

"I know," Benny said, though he wasn't absolutely sure of that.

Lacerra said the winery was going to go up in flames late on Saturday night. Benny said he'd start filling bottles with the wine on Monday, when the restaurant was closed. He reminded Lacerra that he'd need labels for the bottles.

"I got a whole shitload of *La Tache* labels," Lacerra said. "I'll get 'em to you early next week."

"La Tache? That's expensive French wine. Like seven hundred dollars a bottle expensive. Where'd you get the labels from?"

"I've had them for a long time. A friend of mine who's a printer made them up for me. My cousin and me been doing a little switching on our own for a while. The labels work, too. Didn't get no complaints."

Benny and Lacerra ended their conversation, and on Saturday Benny tried to catch up on things at Pazzo Oeuf. The time that

Joey and he had taken off had taken a small toll on the place. They were short on supplies—which Benny ordered at once—and Benny had to create specials based on the limited supplies the place did have and what he could get his hands on on Saturday.

He was busy as hell that day and only thought about Lacerra when he saw the wine stocked in the basement of the restaurant or in his living room at home.

On Sunday morning, he woke up early, walked to Third Avenue, and bought a *Daily News*. He sat at his kitchen table, drank a cup of coffee, and opened the newspaper.

There was an article on the winery fire on page fifteen. There weren't many details, since the fire had occurred late Saturday night, but it did report that the local fire marshal did *not* call the fire suspicious. In fact, the official commented on what a successful winery it had been and that it was a great loss to the community.

Benny figured there'd be a follow-up article in Monday's paper. So he skipped to the sports section and read an article discussing the pros and cons of free agents. Then he checked the point spread for a number of professional football games. If and when he had a moment, he'd make a few wagers.

He spent the rest of the day at the restaurant. Teena, he thought, looked particularly great that day. So during those moments when neither he nor she was particularly busy—which weren't all that many—he discussed how great she was doing and how pleased he was with her.

She was delighted to hear it. And she told him she hoped that some time he could give her some kitchen tips.

"I can't fry an egg without screwing it up," she laughed.

Benny said he'd be happy to teach her anything she wanted to learn or answer any questions she might have.

She said she did have one question, although it had nothing to do with cooking.

"What is it?" Benny asked.

"Well, what's with all the empty wine bottles downstairs?" she asked. "I heard Joey downstairs before you got in, and I think he must have tripped over them, so I went down to see if he was alright. They're all over the place. Isn't that . . . I don't know . . . a fire hazard or something?"

Benny smiled, though he knew he'd have to lie to her—or at least stretch the truth a bit. "They'll be out of there this week. They just sort of pile up, you know?"

She seemed confused. "So why don't you just throw them out in the garbage?"

Benny thought fast. "There's all those recycling laws, you know. We can't just throw them out. They have to go to a recycling center."

"Oh," she exclaimed, and it seemed she was going to ask another question, but a customer was waving for her attention, so she went back to work.

Benny returned to the kitchen and made sure his assistants were doing what they were supposed to be doing. He felt lousy about lying to Teena, but he wanted to protect her from the whole Lacerra affair. That, and he didn't want her to know about his ties to people she might consider unsavory.

She never brought up the subject again that day. The following day Pazzo Oeuf was closed. By the end of the week, most of the wine and the empty bottles were gone from the restaurant.

Benny, Joey, and assorted cousins began working after hours to "transfuse" the stuff. On Tuesday, a UPS package arrived at the restaurant. In it were a few hundred phony labels for the expensive imported wine, and during the rest of the week the wine "assembly line" filled and labeled bottle after bottle with the Long Island–produced wines. Benny supervised the operation and assigned everyone involved a task. He and Joey actually "transfused" the wine. One of Joey's cousins was put in charge of gluing the labels on and sealing the bottles, after Benny and Joey showed him how to do it. Joey, Benny decided, would make most of the drop-offs.

When they had enough bottles to fence, Benny called his old clients. Some of them were more than willing to buy the "expensive" wines at cut-rate prices. Others, who might have been privy to Lacerra's past as Benny's supplier and also privy to Lacerra's current tenuous situation with the higher-ups, had to be persuaded. Benny denied the wine had any connection to his former supplier, and some of them believed him. Others flat out said no, and Benny didn't push them too hard.

Benny was pleased and, quite frankly, surprised, when he had moved about three quarters of the wine in just two and a half weeks. He decided he could unload the rest in dribs and drabs, and he kept some for himself and for use at Pazzo Oeuf.

Lacerra had called a couple of times during the process. Benny told him the wine was moving, but didn't go into detail. He didn't tell him that he had collected a total of forty-eight thousand dollars so far. Why should he? he figured. Lacerra hadn't said a word about the insurance money or Benny's cut—not even what Benny's cut would be.

So, Benny thought, I'll hold the cash I have until he *does* say something. It was Benny's own form of temporary insurance.

Then, one Thursday night, Mr. Ranallo came into Pazzo Oeuf with his wife and another couple who Benny didn't know. Benny had been sending him "dividends" from Pazzo Oeuf on a regular basis, and the man seemed to be in a jovial mood. At one point Benny brought a dish of mussels to Mr. Ranallo's table.

"These were just delivered a couple of hours ago," Benny told Mr. Ranallo. "They are the freshest *moules* available this side of the docks."

"*Moules?*" Ranallo asked.

"Mussels," Benny translated.

Ranallo poked the man he was with in the arm with his elbow. "I told you. He's Mr. Fancy."

Benny laughed. "I don't know about that. But I *do* know these are delicious."

He placed the shallow dish on the table. "Enjoy!"

He was about to return to the kitchen, but Mr. Ranallo stood up and followed Benny. Benny noticed and stopped, turning to him.

"I want to have a word with you," Ranallo said. "Can we talk in the back?"

Benny tensed up but tried not to let it show. "Sure."

Once in a private corner of the kitchen, Ranallo announced, "Lacerra's dead. Have you heard?"

Benny didn't have to pretend to be shocked; he *was*. "No. I'm sorry to hear it."

Ranallo just looked at the floor. "He's the second friend I've lost in a year's time."

"I'm sorry."

"I am too. At least to *some extent*. He was ripping me off, Benny. Worse, he was ripping *other people* off, far more important people than me."

Benny just listened. He tried not to react at all.

"Then he tried to pull an insurance scam to get some money and make amends, but it was a case of too little, too late."

Benny just said, "I see."

Ranallo put his hand on Benny's shoulder and asked, "You won't ever be stupid like that, will you?"

Benny fought to keep his composure. "No, sir."

Then Ranallo just stared into his eyes, still holding his shoulder. Benny felt like Ranallo was probing his soul with the intense stare.

"I know you won't, Benny," Ranallo finally said. "You give me my due every month without me even having to ask." He finally let go of the shoulder, then continued. "I know you and Lacerra had a mostly friendly relationship. I'm sorry I had to be the one to tell you the news."

Again, Benny said nothing.

"However," Ranallo said, "business is business. And a family business is built on trust."

"Yes," Benny responded, somewhat awkwardly. "I understand."

Ranallo returned to his table. Benny stood perfectly still—frozen—for a few seconds. Then he noticed Joey a short distance away, staring at him, wondering what was going on. Benny just gave a wave that said everything was okay.

Benny stepped down into the basement to be alone for a minute and try to calm his nerves. He couldn't believe he had gone through all that trouble for . . . nothing. But then he thought about it a little more. After he paid off Joey and the other guys for their labor, and calculated and deducted the cost of the truck rentals and other assorted paraphernalia that was required to "transfuse" and fence the wine, he figured he had still come out ahead.

In fact, he figured, he had cleared close to twenty-five grand off the books. And he still had some bottles left.

Meat

—

Roasted lamb shanks
with orzo, veal reduction, mirepoix, & mascarpone

Various vegetable & starch side dishes

➤ Roasted Lamb Shanks ➤

Flour and sauté lamb shanks.
Remove when brown, and in the same pan sauté leeks
and diced carrots, cooking until soft.
Add red wine.
Add veal stock.
Return lamb shanks to pan.
Cover and put, in oven, cooking until tender.
Remove shanks; strain and press vegetables through sieve.
Reduce until thick.
Cook orzo; toss with mascarpone.
Top with sauce, vegetables and shanks.

➤ Recommended Side Dishes ➤

Raw mushroom risotto
Roasted-garlic mashed potatoes
Potatoes with rosemary
Broccoli rabe
Spinach with garlic
String beans marinara

━ Sixth Course: Meat ━

Exhaustion was setting in.

Benny was goddamned tired.

His feet hurt from standing in the kitchen for hours. Thank God, he thought, that after this next course it would be time for espresso. He felt he could certainly use some.

Oddly, he wasn't hungry.

Not at all.

Maybe it was the fact that he was just too busy preparing the food, serving it, doing every goddamn thing. He had no time to be hungry.

Or maybe it was his nerves. He, like the rest of the guys, he supposed, was a wreck inside, although everyone was doing his best to hide it and act cool.

Benny was checking the readiness of the lamb shanks when all of a sudden he felt dizzy. Maybe those couple of beers he had had earlier weren't agreeing with him. At any rate, *agita* was the last thing he needed now. He pulled a roll of peppermint Tums out of his pocket, peeled back the wrapper, and popped a couple into his mouth, then he sat on a chair for a moment and rested his head in his hands, his elbows on his knees.

He took a deep breath and chewed the chalky antacid tablets.

Could it be me? he wondered. He had put the notion out of his mind for a while, but as the evening progressed, he could sense it creeping back into him.

I've been relatively clean, he assessed.

I haven't really fucked anybody over.

Not really.

Why would they want to whack *me*?

Sure, he realized, he'd had his run-ins with some of the guys sitting in the dining room, especially Palumbo. But breaking each other's balls was a way of life among this circle. He had never been in any real *heavy* battles with any of them. A couple of them he hardly knew. A couple of them he had met a few times. Palumbo—well, he was another story. But even his battles with Palumbo were hardly the stuff of *this* form of retribution. And he doubted that Pally had enough clout with the men who matter anyway.

And then there was Anthony Abbazio.

They had always been good friends.

Always.

There had been times when they hadn't seen each other in six months or a year, but sooner or later their paths would cross, and it was like there had been *no* great amount of time between meetings. They just picked up where they left off the previous time they had met. *That*, in Benny's estimation, was the sign of *true* friendship. It was something that Benny only had with a couple of guys. Joey Arso was another one.

Real honest-to-god compadres. They were hard to come by. But Double A was certainly one.

But then an unpleasant recollection surfaced in Benny's mind. Ranallo had had friends too, including Lacerra. But Lacerra wasn't around anymore. That friendship had lasted only as long as things were done right, as long as the family benefited and was protected.

Friendship was friendship. But business was business.

He wondered if Double A would ever turn on him. He wondered if he could turn on Double A. Or what about *Joey*? Suppose Joey . . .

No. He shook his head and went back to work in the kitchen. I can't think like that, he realized. I'm just getting tired.

I'm just getting fucking *paranoid*.

Benny had never been in any real trouble with any of the underbosses or higher-ups, either. Sure, he had sometimes been caught in the middle of shit that was flying between capos, between different branches of the family. But he had managed *not* to make any important enemies.

At least, he thought he hadn't.

The Tums helped a little . . . But Benny realized that what was bothering his stomach wasn't something that Tums would help. Not even a couple of rolls of Tums would get rid of the knot in his gut.

Benny forked one of the shanks of lamb and placed it in a small dish on the counter. He sliced it down the center, cut a piece of it, stabbed it with his fork, and brought the fork to his mouth. He let the slice of meat sit on his tongue for a couple of seconds before he chewed it.

Oh, yeah, he thought. Another minute and these will be perfect. Just right!

So he removed the rest of the lamb from the oven.

Benny went out into the dining area and collected the dishes from the previous course. The guys seemed calm, and their conversation had certainly quieted. A couple of them were refilling their glasses with wine.

Ianello poured some wine into his glass.

"Hey, Guy," Aspromonte said. "You better take it easy on that vino. What's this, like your sixth or seventh glass?"

"Is it?" Ianello asked. "So what?"

"Nothing. I'm just glad you ain't driving *me* home."

Ianello shot back, "Relax. All Benny's food here will help absorb it. Besides, I'm not even feeling a buzz."

"Okay," Aspromonte said. "If you say so."

Benny removed the last of the dishes and said, "Wine's good for you. Good for the circulation."

"Not if you drink a fucking gallon of it," Ischia added.

"I didn't drink any gallon," Ianello snarled. "Jesus, I'm a big boy. I don't need any mommas monitoring my drinking."

"We just care about you," Ischia said sarcastically.

"Yeah, right," Ianello snapped.

Benny thought he'd help keep things calm, so he said, "Now I'm gonna bring out a lamb dish like no other you've ever had. So all you guys who've been scarfing down the wine, make sure you leave room for *this*. I don't want to see any leftovers."

Double A leaned back and laughed. "Now *there's* someone who sounds like momma."

"Looks and cooks like her too," Pally added, smiling when he said it. Then, remembering the truce he and Benny had called and thinking Benny might take the remark the wrong way, he added, "Cooks *better* than *my* momma did, anyway."

Benny let the comment slide. A moment later he reemerged from the kitchen with a large dish. "If there are any vegetarians here tonight, I pity them," he said.

He placed the dish in the center of the table, said "Bon appétit!" and returned to the kitchen.

Benny was doing extremely well at Pazzo Oeuf. He was more than comfortable financially and could afford most of the things he wanted. He bought his parents a house in St. Petersburg, Florida, where they could spend the winters or reside year round if they wanted to. They were thrilled, but for the time being they opted to stay in the Florida house only from January to May.

Benny was also earning a solid reputation as a chef. Pazzo Oeuf was named one of the top five restaurants in Brooklyn by two different magazines. Several of his recipes were featured in newspapers.

Celebrities began visiting his restaurant, and Benny took that as a *true* sign that he had arrived. If they were traveling to Brooklyn to dine at his place, then *that* was something. First San Butera, who sounded a lot like Louie Prima and sang with the Witnesses, came by, and then Dean Martin showed up one night, and Benny couldn't believe it. Nor could he believe the hordes of people who accompanied the entertainer, mostly musicians who were on tour with him. After the dinner, Dino shook Benny's hand and told him that the meal could rival *any* he'd eaten anywhere. He autographed a photo and gave Benny a half-dozen tickets to his show at Westbury Music Fair the next night.

The gift of those tickets, Benny realized, was an opportunity Benny had been looking for. At closing time, after Dino and his entourage had left, Benny approached Teena, who was getting ready to go home.

"Hey, Teena," Benny said. "Mr. Martin gave me tickets to his show tomorrow night. Could I interest you in going?"

Teena's answer puzzled him for a moment. "Are you sure? Who'll work tomorrow night for me? And who'll work for *you*?"

Benny laughed. "You let me worry about that." Then he added, gently, "I'd really like you to go with me."

"Is this a *date*?" she asked.

"Sure," Benny responded. "Unless you're against dating the boss. In that case, it's *not* a date."

She just looked at him for a moment. Then she said, "Sure. I'd love to go."

"I'll pick you up at six thirty."

"I'll be ready."

She grabbed her pocketbook and headed for the door. But before she left, she turned, looked at Benny, and broke into a big smile.

The show was great the next night. But even better was the time he spent at Teena's apartment after the show. Benny learned a lot about her during the couple of hours he was there.

He recalled that Teena had aspirations of breaking into show business as a dancer. There had been a few nights along the way since he had hired her that she didn't come in to work, but they weren't often, so Benny never complained, even though he doubted that she was ill. He had agreed to that when she first agreed to work for him, and he kept his word, although it bothered him for both personal and business reasons when she was out.

He learned that she was from Virginia, and that just helped Benny fashion his image of her as a Southern belle, a gorgeous, timid creature from some old Hollywood movie about the days of the Civil War. In thinking that, Benny was both right and wrong. She *was* gorgeous, there was no doubt about that.

But Teena was far from timid.

Benny found that out as she initiated the rolling and tumbling on her couch and floor after a couple of drinks. She was passionate, she was earthy, and she hadn't the slightest hesitation in trying to get what she wanted.

That night, right there in her apartment, she wanted Benny. There was no doubt in his mind—or in hers—that that was true. Benny enjoyed every minute with her like this. He had been with sexually aggressive women before, but most of the time their aggression turned him off. But not with Teena. Her assertiveness was controlled. It didn't smother Benny, didn't make him feel less of a man. It was somehow *emp*owering rather than *over*powering.

It was hot. But Benny felt something with Teena he had never felt before. It went beyond the passion, beyond the kissing and the touching and the nakedness and the heat of it all.

Benny was in love. And, he learned, as the two of them held each other afterward, so was she.

Teena told him that she had fallen in love with him over time. It hadn't been, she said, one of those "love at first sight" scenarios from bad movies. It had happened slowly, one step at a time. The way he had spoken to her that first day at Café Bari and the day he had asked her to work for him. The way he treated her with respect at Pazzo Oeuf. And then she began to really watch him, she revealed. His creativity—genius was the word she used—in the kitchen truly impressed her. The combination of patience and firmness he had with his kitchen staff. The way he cared about *everything* in his restaurant, and the way he had turned a run-of-the-mill neighborhood Italian restaurant into a showplace for fine food and a showcase for his talents.

When Benny left her place in the small hours of the morning, he felt wonderful. He felt fulfilled. He felt satisfied. He felt like he had damn near everything he had ever wanted. And now just about all of his needs were being met.

Just about.

Something was still missing, although it took Benny a few days after the night with Teena to realize what it was.

Teena was exciting enough, and they continued to see each other steadily, making love at either his or her apartment every couple of nights. There were times at the restaurant when Benny just wanted to have her right there, right then. But he restrained himself (except for one night after the place had closed, and he could tell that she just wanted it—and he was correct).

It wasn't sex or love that was missing from Benny's life.

It was a different sort of excitement, one that took him a while to realize had been missing.

It was the rush of pulling a scam.

Despite the tension and the very real dangers that went with it, executing the art of the scam had its rewards. There was the financial gain, of course, but it was more than that. It was knowing you had put one over on someone. It was the satisfaction of conning someone and the feeling of superiority that went with it.

It had become a part of Benny's life over the previous couple of years. But recently, with all his legitimate success, his thriving restaurant, and his growing reputation in the world of fine cuisine, Benny had neither the time nor the inclination for a scam.

Now, however, he longed for this missing ingredient in his recipe for *complete* happiness and satisfaction.

So he thought about it and, after a couple of days, turned to Joey Arso once again to help him make some easy money.

Joey was just as eager—more, perhaps—for some adventure in his life. He, after all, did not have a talent that was being recognized by others in the field, nor a business of his own, nor, for that matter, a woman like Teena in his life. It wasn't that Joey was unhappy or dissatisfied with his job as "business manager" of Pazzo Oeuf. On the contrary, he was more than happy to do whatever Benny asked him to do, whether that was checking deliveries, making up the wait staff's schedules, or whatever. But he, even more than Benny, felt just a bit out of place being so respectable.

Together they cooked up a scheme.

Benny thought it up, then ran the idea by Joey, who laughed when he heard it but agreed to it because he thought "it would be fun." Benny himself was not too sure about the fun part but thought they could pull it off. Just the two of them.

So five days after they came up with the scam they were in the midst of the operation. It was about eleven o'clock in the morning and someone was ringing the downstairs bell of Benny's apartment to be let into the building.

As planned, Benny stepped to his living room window and peered down into the street. The delivery truck was there, double-parked outside his building, its hazard lights blinking. Parked across the street was a maroon Chevy Malibu. Joey was behind the wheel, his arm hanging out the open window.

Again, the bell rang.

Again, Benny didn't answer it.

Instead, he put on his jacket, stepped into the hallway of the fifth floor of his building, and locked the door behind him. Then he felt inside the jacket pocket for reassurance. He felt better when he realized the pistol was in the pocket, right where he had put it earlier that morning.

Benny rang for the elevator. He heard its motor hum and could feel a slight vibration in the building as the elevator car made its way up the shaft.

When the car arrived, he stepped inside. The door closed, Benny pushed the Lobby button, and the car descended. Benny reached into the other pocket of the jacket and felt the rubber mask.

He was all set.

It was time to get this thing done.

When Benny stepped into the lobby, he could see the delivery man, a clipboard in his hand, speaking to an elderly woman just outside the building. Peering past them, across the street, Joey was obviously bopping his head to something he was listening to on the car radio.

Benny stepped outside in the bright but chilly autumn morning air.

"Can't say I know the party you're looking for," the gray-haired old woman said to the deliveryman. "Cocoa, you said?"

"*La*coco," he corrected. "Apartment E5."

The woman shook her head. "Never heard of him."

Benny stepped past them and crossed the street.

"Thanks, anyway," the driver said.

Benny got into the passenger seat of the Chevy Malibu. Joey

smiled a wide grin at him, still moving his head to the song on the radio. It was "Shattered" by the Rolling Stones.

The driver got back into his truck and wrote something on the paper attached to the clipboard.

Benny lowered the radio as Jagger sang.

"You packing?" Benny asked.

"Packed and loaded," Joey answered, strangely cheerfully. Then he tapped the top front of his trousers.

The truck's side was decorated with a panel-long picture of a white dish containing a meal of mashed potatoes, broccoli, and, most noticeably, a thick steak that had been sliced through once, revealing the beef's perfect pink center. Above the picture was the company name—Exceptional Steaks—and the company's motto: "World-famous steaks . . . superlative taste . . . delivered to your door."

Then the driver started the truck's engine and slowly drove up the block.

Joey started his car too.

"Where'd you get the car?" Benny asked.

"From Kingsway Car Service."

"You get it from Bobby?"

"No. I got it from Cappy."

"Who's Cappy?"

"Cappy's . . . I don't know his real name. Just Cappy. You know Cappy."

Benny pointed to the truck. "Pull out, but don't get too close."

Joey followed the steak delivery truck.

"Anyhow, Cappy lent me the car," Joey continued.

"These license plates legit?" Benny asked.

"Cappy took off the plates and put these on."

Benny asked, "He doesn't know what we're doing, does he? I mean, you didn't tell this Cappy anything?"

"Nah. I just told him he might want to change the plates."

"That's all you said?"

"Yeah."

Joey turned the corner. The truck was about a hundred feet in front of them.

"I still can't figure out who Cappy is."

Joey laughed. "I'm tellin' you, you know Cappy."

"That his real name?"

"Nah. Something like Capreda or Capraro or something."

"Don't know him," Benny insisted. He hoped Joey hadn't fucked up.

"You *do* know him," Joey said. "I'm telling you."

"From where?"

Joey thought about it, all the time keeping the truck in sight.

"I'll tell you where," he went on. "You remember one time— now this is years ago—you and me and Double A went to that basketball game and got into a fight with a bunch of guys from the other school. They were chucking shit at us all night. You remember that?"

Benny thought for a moment. "That game against Holy Cross?"

"Yeah, we were seniors. They were a bunch of douche bags who were trying to impress their girlfriends."

"And we got into this massive fistfight in the parking lot after?"

"That's it," Joey smiled.

"So who was Cappy?" Benny asked.

"He was the guy who broke up the fight."

Benny had to think about it. After a minute, he thought he knew who Joey was talking about.

"You don't mean the kid who pulled that drum out of his car?"

"Yeah, him."

"The guy who smashed a bass drum over that guy's head?"

"Yeah," Joey laughed. "Him! He was in our class."

"He was?"

"Yeah."

"He was in a band back then. Played the high schools all the time."

"His name is Cappy?"

"Yeah. Anyway, that's what he's called."

"That's who you got the car from?"

"It's cool," Joey said. "Cappy's a great guy." Joey noted the concern on Benny's face. "I'm telling you, everything's copacetic. Cappy's good people."

Benny saw the truck turn onto Third Avenue under the shadow of the elevated Gowanus Expressway.

"Keep up with him," Benny said. "Unless he turns off Third Avenue, a few blocks from here get ahead of him and block him. Make him stop. We'll do it there."

"Got ya!" Joey said.

The truck remained on the avenue. The further downtown it went, the less residential the neighborhood became. A few stores lined the avenue, and there was plenty of traffic, but not many pedestrians walked the streets. The elevated parkway above cast a shadow that seemed to keep people off the streets—except those who *had* to be there.

"You know that porno place down here?" Benny asked.

"Yeah, I know it," Joey answered. "Down about a mile?"

"Yeah. Stop him a few blocks after that."

"You got it."

Joey stepped on the gas, got in the left lane of the two-lane avenue, and passed the Exceptional Steak truck. A few blocks later the car passed the sign that said "PLEASURE BARN—TURN HERE!"

"It's pretty quiet down here," Benny noted. "Do it two blocks down."

Joey just smiled and looked at the truck behind him in the rearview mirror. He moved the Malibu back into the right lane, directly in front of the truck. When they passed the second intersection—a block completely kept in shadow by the highway above them, with no pedestrians within eyeshot—Joey slammed on the brakes.

The truck driver hit his brakes too, and the sound of whining, grating metal resounded off the surrounding buildings. In his rearview mirror, Joey could see the driver cursing.

"Should I get out?" Joey asked Benny.

"Hold it," Benny answered. "Just wait a minute. Let's see what he does."

Benny's instincts were correct. The driver got out of his truck in a hurry and walked quickly up to the car.

"Here he comes," Joey said. "Put your mask on." They both put on rubber animal face masks that hid their faces, covering the area from their foreheads to their mouths. Then both he and Benny pulled their guns out but kept them out of sight.

The driver walked up to the driver door and banged on the window with his fist. His face was beet red. Joey lowered the window.

"What the fuck is wrong with you?" the driver asked. "You just stop like that? You some kind of asshole or what?"

By way of answer, Joey raised his pistol to the man's chest. Benny's was pointed at him too.

"*You're* the asshole, asshole!" Joey said, shoving the tip of the gun barrel against the driver's chest.

"What the . . . ?" the driver reacted, both to the guns and the face masks.

"Get in the backseat," Benny shouted from within. *"Now!"*

"You guys are kidding me, right?" the driver asked nervously.

"Get in the fucking car," Benny repeated.

The frightened driver did as he was told. Once sitting, he saw that Benny had a gun too. He left the back door of the Chevy open.

"Close the door," Benny ordered.

"Yeah," Joey added. "Whaddaya live in, a barn or something?"

The driver closed the door and said, "What do you want? I don't have any money except for maybe thirty dollars in my wallet."

Benny waved the gun at the man. "Keep your money. Give me the keys to the truck."

"You're gonna take my truck?"

"Shut up and give me the keys."

The driver handed them to Joey, who had his hand bent backward over his shoulder.

"Go do it," Benny said.

"As good as done," Joey answered. Then he got out of the car, took off the mask and shoved it in his pocket, and walked back to the truck.

Benny held his gun on the driver. Sweat was beginning to roll down the man's face, and the drops beaded in his thick mustache.

"You just sit there and shut up and keep your hands where I can see them, and I won't have to pop you," Benny said sternly. "You understand what I'm saying?"

"I understand."

Benny glanced past the driver, through the rear window. He saw Joey get out of the truck and walk to the back of the vehicle. Then he heard the grating sound of the cargo door being opened.

Keeping the gun aimed at the driver, Benny reached over near the steering wheel and flipped the lever that opened the car's trunk. The driver suddenly got very nervous.

"You . . . you aren't gonna put me in there, are you?" he said. "I'm claustrophobic."

Benny shook his head. "Why would we do that?"

"Please don't," the driver continued.

"Shut up, already!" Benny said, agitated.

Then both men in the car heard something thud in the trunk. Because the trunk door was open and blocking the view beyond the rear window, neither could see what was going on. But Benny knew Joey was putting the cartons of frozen steaks into the trunk.

"You're stealing the meat?" the driver asked. "I can't believe it."

Benny grew annoyed and pointed the gun like he meant business. "I don't give two shits *what* you believe. Just shut up before I lose my patience. Just shut up."

Traffic whizzed by, but hardly a pedestrian could be seen. Benny kept an eye out for cop cars, but didn't see any. He assumed Joey was doing the same.

More thuds resounded from the trunk. Finally, after a few more minutes and several more thumps from the back of the car,

Joey shut the trunk. Then he got back in the car behind the wheel, his mask back on his face.

"All set," Joey said.

"What are you guys gonna do with those steaks?" the driver asked.

"We're gonna shove 'em up your ass," Joey said, then snickered at his own remark.

"I'm gonna lose my job for this."

Benny said, "I told you to shut up."

"I need my job, man," the driver went on. "I'll lose my job and my wife will walk out on me and . . ."

"*Shut up!!*" Benny said.

"You guys are a couple of scumbags, you know that?"

Benny shifted his weight so that he was practically kneeling on his seat. He leaned over and pressed the end of the gun barrel against the driver's forehead.

"I was just gonna let you go," he said. "But you are one obnoxious fuck, you know that?"

"Don't shoot me," the driver pleaded.

Then Joey tapped Benny on the arm. "Hey, let's split. I see a flashing light down further on third. Can't tell if it's cops or not."

"Turn the corner," Benny said. "Go halfway up the block."

"What about my truck?" the driver said.

"Fuck your truck," Joey answered, and slowly drove up a one-way street toward Fourth Avenue. Midblock, he stopped.

Benny said to the driver. "Get out of the car."

"What?" the driver asked.

"You heard me. Get out of the car."

"Can I have the keys to the truck?"

"Just get out."

"But how will I get out of here? This is a shitty spic neighborhood."

Benny had had it. "Get out of this fucking car or spics are the last things you'll have to worry about." To emphasize his point, he cocked the gun.

"Okay, I'm going." The driver jumped out of the car, constantly eyeing the gun Benny had pointed at him. He slammed the door shut.

Joey saw that the light on the corner was green, so he stepped hard on the accelerator and took off.

From a distance they heard the driver screaming after them. "You'll get yours, you motherfuckers!"

As they drove through the intersection and up the next block, Joey said, "We *already* got ours. Right, Benny?" He raised his right hand so that Benny could high-five him, which he did.

"Right." Benny removed his mask and said, "You can take that thing off *your* face too, you know."

"Oh, yeah," Joey said. He peeled his mask off also.

They drove in silence for a while, then Benny asked, "How many boxes did you get?"

"About twenty-four, I think."

"How many steaks in a box?"

"A dozen, I think."

"That's close to six hundred steaks, I think."

"We gonna fence them all?" Joey asked.

"Some," Benny said. "We'll use the rest."

"Cool! That went down like a dream, didn't it?"

"Mostly. But what an obnoxious bastard that guy was."

Joey headed toward Pazzo Oeuf. "You should file a complaint against that guy," he said.

Benny couldn't tell if he was joking or not. But he laughed nonetheless. "You're a pisser. I'm gonna call the company and tell them one of their drivers was obnoxious while we were hijacking his load of meat?"

"Yeah, why not?"

"You crack me up, I swear it."

But Benny couldn't get Joey's idea, as absurd as it was, out of his head. And it ultimately inspired Benny to call the company.

When they arrived at Pazzo Oeuf that midafternoon, Benny brought out a box of black plastic trash bags, which Joey used to wrap the Exceptional Steak cartons in before they were brought into the restaurant. There was no need to let everyone on the staff or in the neighborhood see what these cartons contained or from where they had come.

While Joey unloaded the trunk of the Chevy Malibu, Benny made a phone call from the restaurant. He called the Exceptional Steak Company and bitterly complained that he hadn't received the order of steaks he was promised would be delivered today, and that whoever their delivery guy was in this area, he must be a lazy, inefficient son of a bitch. He, Benny Lacoco, had taken a day off from work to wait for the delivery and the truck had never arrived. He swore he'd never do business with the company again and canceled his order.

Then he hung up. And laughed. Then he told Joey what he had done. And *they* laughed.

Two days later, Benny and Joey had fenced all the steaks they had, except for the few cartons Benny kept for himself for use at the restaurant. He split the money with Joey, and gave him a little extra.

"Throw that Cappy guy a little of that, will you?" he said to Joey. "Whoever he is."

"I told you," Joey started to say, "Cappy was the guy . . ."

"Okay," Benny said. "Okay. I know."

Joey left to return the car, muttering, "Can't believe you don't know Cappy!"

For the rest of the week, one of the specials every night at Pazzo Oeuf was created around steak.

And not just *good* steak.

Exceptional steak.

Coffee and Biscotti

—

French roast coffee
Decaf (if necessary)
Espresso

Seventh Course:
Coffee and Biscotti

Back in the kitchen, Benny turned on the coffee machine. He didn't know if *he* himself actually would have any; he felt jittery enough without the added caffeine. Not knowing exactly what was going to go down soon was making him feel nervous.

He hated being in limbo, and that was exactly where he felt he was. Throughout his life, any time he had thought he might be in trouble he had always preferred to meet the possible confrontation head on. Avoiding it was stupid and only delayed a resolution, good or bad. And, most of all, he hated being in a position of *not knowing*.

On the other hand, some coffee and a couple of biscotti would keep him alert and keep him going until this night's resolution arrived.

Yeah, he figured, when the coffee was ready, he'd sit with the guys and have a cup or two himself.

In the dining area, the guests were still bullshitting each other with tales of their various adventures and conquests. Many of these stories Benny had heard before, either first- or secondhand.

They didn't interest him much, nor did he feel like joining in at the moment.

But he entered the dining room anyway and began to collect the dishes from the previous course.

Double A asked him, "You ever gonna sit down, Benny? You're like a one-man show here. Relax for a couple of minutes and join us."

Benny smiled, piling the dishes on a tray.

"I've got coffee and biscotti coming next," he answered. "I'll take a break when I bring that out."

"Good," Aspromonte added. "You look tired, man. You eat anything yourself tonight?"

"Yeah. I've been nibbling in the back, you know, here and there."

Sapienza started to say something, but his comment was interrupted by a crash from outside. It sounded like a car accident.

All of the guys walked to the front window. It was as if they were all desperate for something—anything—to distract them from the underlying tension that was building.

Ianello spotted the car first.

"Look," he said, pointing down the avenue. "Poor son of a bitch crashed into a telephone pole."

"Head on, from the looks of it," Di Pietro added.

"He hit anyone's car?" Pally asked, struggling to see past the other guys. "I mean, any of ours?"

"No," Sapienza responded. "Just drove clear into that telephone pole."

"Then fuck him," Pally exclaimed and returned to his chair.

"Someone should call an ambulance," Double A said. "That was a pretty nasty hit."

"Someone else'll do it," Pally shot back. "You want the cops getting *your* witness statement?"

Benny hated to admit it, but Pally was right. This was not a night any of the boys should get involved with the cops *at all*.

"The guy got out of the car," Ischia commented, still observing the situation from the window. "All on his own. He can't be hurt that bad."

"And here comes the law," Sapienza said, pointing to a police car arriving on the scene. "Let's get back to our seats and away from the window."

Everyone recognized this as sound advice and retook their seats.

But Benny lingered by the window. He wasn't looking at the scene of the accident. He had spotted someone lingering in the shadows of the three- and four-story buildings on the other side of the street.

There was a man smoking a cigar outside Cobbler's across the avenue. He was standing in the darkness, but Benny thought he recognized him, though he couldn't be sure.

Then the big man—broad-shouldered and tall—tossed the cigar in the street and opened the door to Cobbler's. The light from inside the bar illuminated his face for the few seconds before he entered the place.

It was the Big O.

Oppido.

Benny couldn't remember his first name. Was it Vinny? Aldo? What the hell was it?

He just couldn't recall. It didn't matter, really. What *did* matter was that wherever the Big O was some nasty shit was sure to happen.

There was *no* way he was just socializing with the customers in Cobbler's.

Oppido's reputation as an enforcer was legendary. Even families on the West Coast knew of him. And even guys way up at the top were nervous when they were in his presence and therefore treated him with kid gloves.

No one wanted their balls cut off and shoved in their mouths, which was reputed to be the Big O's "signature." That and the sawed-off shotgun he carried around.

"Hey, Benny," Sapienza called out. "Can't get enough of that accident, huh? You one of those guys always slowing down traffic on the Belt Parkway because you gotta gawk at accidents?"

"Nah," Benny responded, trying to keep cool. "I just thought I saw somebody I recognized."

He walked past the men, most of whom were sitting down once again.

"I'll get the coffee. Anyone want espresso instead?"

A few of the guys said they would prefer espresso, so Benny said he'd bring it out and retreated back into the kitchen. He fumbled around for a few minutes, checking and rechecking the brewed beverages. Benny was stalling for time, trying to compose himself.

The sight of the Big O had shaken him. In his mind, little question remained that something *big* was going to go down tonight.

Some*thing* or some*one*.

The Big O didn't just *happen* to be in the neighborhood.

Benny wanted to let Double A know who he had seen, but he didn't want to tell anyone else. After all, Double A was his friend.

But then a phrase echoed in Benny's memory: "Business is

business." And he was torn for a few minutes, weighing the options of telling Abbazio or keeping his mouth shut.

Ultimately, the echoing words made the difference. As much as he liked Double A, as much as he valued him as a true friend, *business was business*.

That was all there was to it.

Benny eventually brought out the cups and saucers and silverware, and the coffee and espresso. He went back into the kitchen and returned with a pitcher of half-and-half and a bowl of sugar. Last, he placed a large dish of biscotti in the center of the table.

Then he pulled a chair up to the table to join the crowd. He moved the chair to a spot at the table where he could keep an eye out across the street. Doing this didn't make much sense, he realized, but it did, for some reason, make him feel better.

He sat at the table between Aspromonte and Di Pietro. Under more normal circumstances, he probably would have sat next to Double A.

But he didn't feel quite right about that at this particular time.

Although he had joined the company at the table, Benny's thoughts drifted elsewhere. They wandered off into the not-too-distant past.

He remembered the night—and the *sight*—as if it were yesterday.

There was a knock at his apartment door. Then the doorbell rang. Benny had fallen asleep for a while after watching a rerun episode of *Wiseguy*. He thought he had heard the knock but didn't pay any attention to it, figuring it had been the television he had forgotten to shut off. But when the doorbell rang loud and clear, he knew better.

He got out of bed, cursing to himself, and approached the door slowly and silently. Who the hell could this be? he wondered. Then the bell sounded again.

He looked through the peephole and recognized Joey standing outside in the hallway. He had his hand pressed against his face.

Benny unlocked the door and opened it.

Joey quickly stumbled into the apartment and fell into a nearby chair. His face was all bloody, and he was trying to stop the blood from pouring out of his nose.

"What the fuck happened to you?" Benny asked.

Joey didn't answer. His eyes were rolling around in their sockets, and Benny thought his friend might pass out at any minute.

"Don't move," he said, going into the kitchen.

"Ugghh!" Joey groaned, his words slurred. "I think my nose is broken."

Benny returned to him with a washcloth filled with ice cubes. He placed it in Joey's hand and lifted the hand to the base of the bloody nose.

"You want some water or something?" Benny asked. "You feel like you're gonna pass out?"

Joey shook his head. He pressed the washcloth against his face.

Benny looked Joey over. There were bruises on the sides of his face, a cut on his forehead, and the top of his right ear was bleeding where there was a slight tear. Joey's bottom lip was split and swollen.

"Someone do this to you?" Benny asked.

Joey nodded. He moved the washcloth beneath his nostrils and tilted his head back.

"Who was it? Do you know?"

Joey pulled the washcloth away from his face so he could

answer. "Yeah, I know. One of them at least." Then he pressed the ice back against his face.

"That bleeding stopping?" Benny asked.

Joey nodded, but kept the ice where it was anyway.

"You hurt anywhere else? I mean, besides the face?"

Joey shook his head, then pulled the washcloth away from his face. "Just bruises," he said. "I guess I got off easy." He handed the bloody cloth to Benny.

Benny took it and threw it in the kitchen sink. When he returned, he took a closer look at Joey. His nose *was* broken. And the flesh around his eyes—particularly under them—was red and puffy.

"You want me to get a doctor?" Benny asked.

"No," Joey said.

"Your nose is practically pointing east, man."

Benny hadn't meant that as a joke, but Joey laughed for a second anyway. "Don't make me fuckin' laugh, man. I'll start bleeding again."

"Sorry."

Joey let his hands fall to his sides. "This ain't the first time my nose has been broken."

"I know," Benny said. "I broke it the first time when I beaned you with a softball in seventh grade."

"Yeah."

"You fixed it yourself. Shoved your beak right into place again," Benny noted. "The fucking cracking noise it made practically turned my stomach."

"Yeah," Joey said. Then he warned, "Hold onto your stomach. I'm gonna do it again."

"Oh, shit!"

Benny braced himself and turned his head, but he heard the cracking sound anyway. He also heard Joey groan.

But then he heard Joey say, "At least it gets easier every time. This is number five, I think. I lost count."

Benny got him a shot of Scotch, which Joey downed in a gulp.

"Sure you don't need a doctor?"

"Yeah. I'll take another hit of this shit though."

Benny refilled the glass, and again Joey drank it down.

"Any broken bones or anything?" Benny asked.

"I'm bruised up, that's all. Those guys couldn't throw a *real* beating on their grandmother."

"Who was it? What the hell happened?"

"I went down to Ludlow's, down in Sheepshead Bay."

Benny winced in disgust. "What for? How can you eat that shit?"

"Hey, I just felt like some fried clams and a cold Bud. That okay with you?"

"Whatever."

"So two guys jump me when I head back to my car. Right out in the street. Caught me off guard, too, or I woulda kicked them into next fucking week."

"Were they white guys?"

"One was. I recognized him as he was taking jabs at my face. Musta had brass knuckles on. I was seeing fucking stars, man. The other guy—a shine with a big gold earring—held me from behind."

"Why'd they rough you up?"

"Damned if I know. Probably just rolled me for the cash. They took the couple of hundred I had in my pocket. Didn't take my wallet or credit cards or anything else. Threw the wallet at me when they left."

"So then you drove all the way here from Ludlow's?"

"After I came to, I did. Got blood all over my car."

Benny patted his friend on the shoulder. "At least you're okay."

"Alive, maybe," Joey concurred. "I don't know how okay I am. I'm sore from my head to my fuckin' feet."

"You want to crash here tonight?" Benny asked.

Joey turned and tried to look into the bedroom. "You got Teena here tonight?"

"Not tonight."

"What happened? You guys have a fight?"

Benny laughed. "No. She was tired and wanted to go home to sleep."

"Really?"

"Hey, everybody needs a day off once in a while," Benny added.

"Yeah," Joey said. "That reminds me. I'm taking off tomorrow."

"Take a few days off," Benny suggested. "Until you feel better. And until you *look* better."

Joey stood up slowly. "I'm gonna head home."

"You sure?"

"Yeah. Just let me wash my face."

Joey went into the bathroom, and Benny heard the sound of the faucet running. When Joey came back out into the living room, he looked better. No blood remained on his face, and his hair was combed. But his face was still red and puffy, especially his nose.

"You're welcome to stay," Benny reassured him.

"I know. I just wanna get home. Then, tomorrow, I'm gonna go after those motherfuckers."

"Hey, why don't you wait?" Benny suggested. "There's no hurry."

"Yes, there is. That Raffanello ain't getting away with this."

"Raffanello?" Benny repeated. "*Ernie* Raffanello?"

"Yeah, that prick!"

"*He* jumped you?"

"It was him. That fuckin' junkie bastard. I'm gonna cut out his heart and shove it up his junkie ass."

Benny tried to calm Joey down. "Hey, right now go home and sleep. And give me a call tomorrow. Forget about Raffanello for now."

"Yeah, okay."

Joey limped to the door, and as he exited, he said, "Thanks, Benny. Sorry to bother you so late at night."

"No problem," Benny responded. "Talk to you tomorrow."

A few minutes later, Benny fell back to sleep, again with the television on.

Late the next afternoon, Benny got a phone call from Joey. Benny was giving his staff instructions on the preparation of the evening's specials.

"Hey! What're you doing?" Joey asked.

"A better question," Benny replied, "would be *how* are *you* doing?"

"I'm sore. And swollen. But I'm going after Raffanello."

"What, now?"

"Now."

"All by yourself? Don't be crazy. Wait until tonight. I'll go with you."

"I wanna go now."

"Slow down, will you?" Benny said. "Where are you gonna find him?"

"At his old man's store, that's where."

"Where's that?"

"That music store on Nostrand Avenue. I forget the name of it."

"A record store?"

"No. You know, a music store. Drums, guitars, and that shit. He lives in the apartment above the store."

"Oh, yeah," Benny said. "I *do* know. I forgot that Raffanello used to think he was God's gift to music."

"The stupid prick thought he was gonna be the next Jimi Hendrix."

"I remember."

"Turned out to be just another asshole," Joey commented. "Though he is gonna be like Jimi Hendrix—*dead!*"

Benny insisted that Joey hold off on taking any retaliatory action. He didn't want Joey to be so impulsive that he went after Raffanello alone and wound up getting in even deeper shit.

It took a couple of minutes of persuasion, but Joey finally agreed. Benny told him to pick him up at 8:30 that night at the restaurant and they'd work something out together.

Benny wanted to protect his friend, but his reason for wanting to go with Joey was more complicated than that. Benny had no great love for Raffanello either, but it was the excitement that he craved.

The revenge.

The laying on of a beating on someone who really deserved it.

Benny found himself thinking about it the whole day. He had a hard time concentrating on the restaurant or anything or anyone in it.

Except for Teena, of course.

Then he remembered that he and Teena were supposed to go out for drinks and, after, go to his place for a romantic evening together.

He thought about calling Joey back and asking him to wait until tomorrow night to go after Raffanello. But he didn't. He was afraid that Joey wouldn't be able to wait and would hunt his attacker down without him. And, besides, the kind of excitement Teena could give him, he figured, he could get *after* he went out with Joey.

So, instead, in the middle of the afternoon, during a slow stretch of time at the restaurant, he asked Teena if he could meet her at her place around one o'clock.

"One A.M.?" she asked. "Aren't you closing up?"

"No," Benny answered. "I have to leave early. Got some business to attend to. But I should be back by one."

"Really?" Teena said with a slight snarl in her voice. "What am I supposed to do? Just wait up until you decide to show?"

"I'll be there at one."

"What kind of business could you have at that hour of the night?" she wanted to know.

"It's not another woman," Benny said. "If that's what you're thinking."

"I'm not thinking anything," she snapped. "Except that you're starting to get a little weird on me. You know, I don't mind the gambling and all that stuff, even though I don't particularly understand *that* addiction. But how can you let whatever it is cut into *our* time? I just don't get it."

Benny wanted to continue the discussion, but customers entered the place, and Teena hurried over to them, clearly, Benny thought, to get away from him.

He walked back into the kitchen, first thinking "fuck her," but that thought rapidly changed into something closer to "what's the big deal?"

They didn't really speak much again that day until Joey came to get Benny at 8:30.

Benny spotted Joey's car outside.

So did Teena.

And when Benny asked her if he'd see her later, her reply was a sarcastic "Not tonight. I have a headache. I think it was brought on by *gambling*."

Annoyed and frustrated, Benny moved past her to Joey's car outside. He sat next to Joey on the front seat.

"The fucker's at the music store," Joey announced. "They close at nine. I called before and checked. Let's pay him a visit as he's closing."

"Let's," Benny echoed. He was anxious to work off some of the anger he was feeling, and he couldn't think of anyone who deserved it more than the bastard who had beat up his friend.

A few minutes later Joey and Benny drove by the Music World store. As they did, they saw Raffanello outside, using a metal pole to pull down the iron grating that would cover the windows and the door of the shop after closing time. Joey quickly pulled into a parking spot around the corner.

He and Benny got out of the car and crept up on Raffanello before he had the grating halfway down to the sidewalk. Joey pushed him hard from behind, and he tumbled into the store, falling face first on the linoleum floor. The pole landed on the floor next to him.

Joey and Benny moved behind him into the store. Benny saw the light switch by the door and flicked the lights off. Joey, meanwhile, kicked Raffanello in the ribs as the man tried to get up.

"Hi, motherfucker," Joey said. "Remember me?"

Benny looked around the store. It appeared that Raffanello was alone. But to make sure, Benny walked into the back office. No one was there. He continued down a short hallway, which led to four small rooms, two on each side. Benny opened the doors, one at a time. Neither of the rooms on the left side contained anything but music paraphernalia: small music stands, sheet music, tiny Fender practice amplifiers, metronomes, and assorted other stuff. Same with the first room on the right.

Before he opened the last door, he heard Raffanello groan as Joey kicked him again in the ribs. The last room contained nothing but a grimy, brown-stained toilet and an equally filthy sink.

When Benny turned, Joey was dragging Raffanello by the feet to the back area. The man struggled to get up, yelling all the time. But Benny grabbed one of his legs and he and Joey together yanked the man into one of the small studio rooms.

"Time for a music lesson, cocksucker!" Joey said angrily.

They tossed Raffanello onto one of the small beige metal folding chairs. Then Joey punched him square in the face.

Raffanello almost fell out of the chair, but Benny picked up a black guitar jack cord and from behind wrapped it around Raffanello's neck and pulled it tight. The long-haired man clutched at the wire, trying to pull it away from his throat. His face started to turn purple.

"You think I didn't know it was you?" Joey asked Raffanello. "You always were a stupid fuck, you know that?"

Benny continued to cut off Raffanello's breath. Joey went back into the main part of the store, but a minute later he was back, a red electric guitar in his hands.

"Gibson," Joey said, reading the decaled brand name on the guitar. Then he asked, "Hey, Benny, you remember The Who? Remember the night we saw them at Madison Square Garden?"

Benny kept the cord wrapped tight around Raffanello's neck. He wasn't sure why Joey was asking him these questions, but he was sure he was going to find out any minute.

And he was correct.

"Remember the guitar player used to do shit like this?"

Joey held the guitar by the neck and began to swing the instrument over and down and around and around.

Then he smashed the wooden back of the guitar across Raffanello's purplish face.

The man's head bent back and wobbled like one of those bobbing-head dogs some people put in their car's rear windows. Blood spurted from his nose and his mouth, and from a huge laceration on Raffanello's face, just below his hairline.

Joey laughed like a lunatic. "I'm telling you, *he* won't get fooled again!" he sang, mockingly. Then, cackling at his own performance, he pinched Raffanello's wallet.

Benny let go of the cord, and the creep slithered out of the chair and onto the floor.

The blood that continued to pour out of his nose began to pool under his head.

Joey looked around the place. Benny knew his friend was

looking to cause more mayhem, but Raffanello was finished. He wasn't moving. He was hardly breathing.

"Let's get out of here," Benny said. "Give me that guitar. I'll wipe your prints off the neck."

"No way," Joey countered, the virtually unharmed solid-body guitar still in his hands. "I'm keeping this baby as a souvenir. Maybe I'll learn how to play it."

Benny didn't argue. Instead, after quickly emptying the cash register, he hurried Joey out of the store. But before they exited, Joey saw a jar filled with colorful, patterned guitar picks.

"I can use these," he said, shoving a handful of them into his pocket.

They got back into their parked car. Joey threw the red Gibson SG onto the backseat. Then he started the car, turned the corner, and they passed Music World.

"Too bad that spade wasn't here," Joey remarked.

Benny looked over at him and asked, "What would you do? Break a guitar over his head too?"

"Maybe," Joey answered. "Or a fuckin' *conga* drum!"

After that evening's incident, Benny realized he had turned a corner in his life. He hadn't been the least bit hesitant about ambushing and pummeling Raffanello. He hadn't been especially nervous during the beating either. And the sight of Raffanello's bloody, suffocating face and split-open head hadn't bothered him much at all.

The bastard had deserved what he got.

During the incident he hadn't thought much—nor did he afterward—about issues of right and wrong, just and unjust, moral and immoral. Giving Raffanello his due wasn't about any of that.

Not at all.

It was about retribution.

It was about inducing fear and not feeling it oneself.

Benny was beginning to enjoy the way of life he had now *truly* become a part of. The money, the respect, the spoils that went to the victor: all of these things he was becoming addicted to.

Raffanello was just a guy some men in the family casually knew. He in no way was truly connected. Nonetheless, word of the incident traveled quickly through several circles. And suddenly Benny was treated with more respect by some of his family associates.

Even Joey, who many important "made men" thought was just some simpleton who did Benny's legwork, was shown some dignity.

Benny stopped hoping to get respect from most people; now he *expected* it. And when it wasn't shown to him, the offender often had hell to pay regardless of whether that person was a perfect stranger or a same-level family member.

In fact, the phrase "a night of action," in Benny's mind, was no longer associated with a night with Teena. It now referred to a night of exacting revenge or reclaiming payments with, and sometimes without, Joey.

Benny was pleased with himself. And many of his associates seemed—at least outwardly—pleased with him, in the same way that a master of an art would be pleased with a successful protégé.

But Teena was dismayed at the "new" Benny. Everything she had admired about him was changing, even disappearing entirely. She thought he had become thoroughly self-absorbed, crude, and lackadaisical about almost everything that used to matter to him.

Especially her.

When Benny did spend time with her—which was becoming less frequent, since he regularly seemed to have "business" late at night to attend to—he was definitely not the man she had gradually become attracted to and greatly admired.

That man took pride in his culinary craft and cared about his work, his establishment, and his staff. *This* man seemed to have lost interest.

That man was charming, a gentleman who treated her with respect, and when he made love to her, she felt special. Much time and care was spent on her, and she was pampered and savored and enjoyed. But *this* man was not the generous, considerate man she first dated and later slept with a few times a week.

She felt like she was being replaced by someone—or something—else. She often wondered if he had someone else, some other woman he would go to when he wasn't with her.

Or maybe it was the gambling.

Maybe he was out somewhere watching the Knicks or the Rangers or the Giants on television, salivating at the thought of his winnings . . . or, more likely, sweating bullets over his losses. A few times he had mentioned losing to her; she rarely heard about him winning.

No, she didn't care much for the current Benny Lacoco, who now seemed to pay attention to her only at the restaurant . . . or when he wanted to get laid.

After weeks of this, she felt she could no longer tolerate the situation or be satisfied with the "new" Benny's on-again off-again attentions. She decided to confront him one night at Pazzo Oeuf, after everyone except Joey had left.

"I think we need to talk," she said to Benny in a serious tone.

Joey heard her words and left the kitchen so Teena could talk privately with his friend.

Benny stood still, leaning on a counter. "What do we need to talk about?"

"About us, Benny, that's what."

"Can't we do this later?"

"Later, when?" she asked, irritated. "When you ring my doorbell at one-thirty in the morning, needing a quicky?"

Benny was caught off guard. "Hey, what's this all about? You unhappy with me all of a sudden?"

"Not all of a sudden," she answered firmly. "It's not sudden at all. But far be it from you to notice."

"Did I *do* something?" he asked. "*Say* something? What?"

Teena put her hands on her hips and stared at him in disbelief.

"It's not some *thing*. It's the combination of things."

"Like what?"

Teena thought he was playing dumb and that made her even more upset.

"Like *this*," she snapped, pulling a handgun from the pocket of Benny's jacket, which was hanging on a hook near the door. "What the hell is *this*? You that deep into gambling debts?"

Benny gently but forcefully took the gun away from her and placed it on the counter. "Don't touch that unless you know how to care for it."

"*Care* for it!" she repeated. "It's a damn *gun*, Benny! You don't *care* for a gun; you care for a woman. At least that's what I thought."

Benny put the gun back in his jacket pocket.

"What the hell do you need that for, anyway?" she wanted to know. "You think you're some sort of mobster or something?"

"For protection," he responded.

"Protection?" she repeated. "From what? From who? You're a *chef*, Benny, not Charles Bronson. Not some character in a gangster movie."

Those words disturbed Benny. He had tried to shield Teena from his less legitimate activities. But apparently he wasn't doing a very good job of it.

"You don't understand," he said. "That's all."

"Oh, I *don't* understand it at all, that's for sure," Teena said. "But I understand certain things. I'm not stupid."

"Of course you're not."

"I understand when I hear you on the phone calling your bookie or whatever he's called, and you're betting thousands on stupid sports. And hell, it's your money. You do what you want with it. But then when I see you on Sunday or Monday, the only things you pay attention to are the games on TV. I might as well not even be there."

"You're making too much of all this," Benny said, making sure his voice was gentle.

She ignored his comment. She was determined to be heard out.

"I also know that you're letting this restaurant turn into just another neighborhood spaghetti stand," she continued. "You used to take pride in it, in your food, in your recipes. Now, you hardly ever do the cooking yourself, because you're too damn busy with . . . whatever it is . . . I really don't want to know."

Joey opened the door just a crack and announced, "Sorry, but we gotta go. We're late."

"I'll be right there," Benny said.

"Don't let me hold you up," Teena said sarcastically, putting on her jacket. "I just hate seeing you waste your talents. You *are* a gifted chef. But instead of focusing on that—or on *me*, for that matter—you'd rather play cops and robbers."

Then she stormed out of the place.

Something inside told Benny that he'd better go after her, but he didn't. Instead, he and Joey went about their business chasing down a bookie who had apparently disappeared with both of their winnings from the week prior.

Thanks to a tip that Joey had received earlier in the day, they eventually found the guy holed up in a ratty Irish bar named Doyle's in Canarsie.

Benny and Joey barged into the seedy, poorly lit place, looked around at the crowd of intoxicated lowlifes, and walked up to the woman behind the bar. She was chopping limes into small half slices.

"Help you gents?" she asked emotionlessly. Her tits were pushed up by a too small bra, and her blouse revealed a generous amount of cleavage.

"We're looking for a guy named Norris," Benny said. "Tim Norris. You know him?"

"Yeah," she said. Benny had to lean forward over the bar to hear her over the loud music blaring from the jukebox. "I think he's still here."

She scoped the place trying to spot him among the wall-to-wall bodies. Thin Lizzy's "The Boys Are Back in Town" cranked out of the jukebox at full volume.

She shrugged her shoulders, but with a raised forefinger indicated that Benny and Joey should wait a minute.

Then the song ended and, taking advantage of the relative quiet, she yelled out, "Norris? Where the hell are ya?"

Benny and Joey turned toward the people gathered in the saloon. Benny spotted someone rising from the table to see what the bartender wanted. The man spotted Benny and Joey, and even from the distance and in the dim light, Benny saw his face go pale.

Benny tapped Joey on the shoulder. "There he is," Benny said.

Joey saw him just as Norris got up from the table and hurried toward the door.

"I'll get him," Joey said, heading toward the exit.

The woman behind the bar grabbed Benny's right arm just above the elbow. "I got a question. What do you guys want with him?"

Benny turned to her and said, "I got a question too. Those tits real?" Then he pulled his arm out of her grasp and followed Joey, who was now outside in the street.

Outside and about one hundred feet away from Doyle's Joey was talking to Norris, who was backing slowly up the street away from him. Norris looked like he was in his late forties. He had the shitty complexion, reddish nose, and sunken eyes of a guy who drank too much too often.

"Shit, man," Joey was saying to him, "I just want to get in on a three-team teaser for Sunday's games. What the hell are you afraid of?"

"Do I know you?" Norris asked. He was obviously drunk, and in his condition should not have been walking backward. He tripped over a chunk of raised sidewalk concrete and fell on his ass.

Joey reached him and helped him to his feet. "You okay?" he asked, holding onto his arm.

Benny walked up beside them and held Norris's other arm.

"Do I know you?" Norris asked again, this time directing the question to Benny.

"We've spoken," Benny answered.

Benny noticed that there was a lot of traffic going by, so he and Joey slowly maneuvered Norris toward their car, which was parked a few feet away.

"Either of you guys got a smoke?" Norris asked.

They had Norris just outside Joey's car. "I have a pack of Camels in the car."

Joey opened the back door and Benny hurriedly shoved Norris in. The man didn't have the time nor the wits to resist. Benny followed in after him and shoved him over on the seat.

Joey got in the driver's seat, started the car, and drove off.

"Hey," Norris said dizzily, his eyes rolling in his head. "Where the hell are we going?"

"It'll cost you eleven thousand two hundred dollars to find out," Benny answered.

Norris looked at him, his eyes barely focused. Then he started laughing. "What the hell are you talking about?" He patted Benny on the knee. "You're a pisser, you know that?"

From the front seat Joey said, "Eleven thousand two hundred dollars. That's what the man said." Then he pulled into a deserted street lined on both sides with warehouses and industrial offices and threw the car into neutral. "Eleven two, you drunken Irish cocksucker. That's what you owe us."

Finally, Norris realized what was happening. Joey's words had permeated the alcoholic haze around his brain. He tried to slip out the driver's side rear door, but Benny prevented this with very little difficulty.

Then Joey got in the backseat, and Norris was sandwiched in-between them.

"Hey, lemme go," the man cried. "I'll get you your money . . . . by tomorrow."

"Yeah," Benny said. "You will!"

Joey took hold of Norris's face, holding him by the chin with his right hand. Then with his left he pulled a switchblade stiletto from his pocket and sliced through the top of Norris' left ear, down about two inches to just above the canal.

Norris tried to scream, but Benny shoved a rag in the man's mouth. Blood poured onto Norris's cheek and dripped from his chin onto his lap. Norris started crying. His sobs were muted by the rag in his mouth. Finally, he slumped down into the seat.

"Tomorrow," Benny repeated. "Eleven thousand, two hundred dollars . . . in cash. You understand?"

Norris just sat there between them.

"You understand?" Joey said. "They can sew that ear up. Next time they'll have to sew it back on. The other one too. You got it?"

Norris nodded feebly.

"Good. You get that money to us," Benny said. "You know what I'm talking about now, don't you?"

Again, Norris nodded.

Benny opened the door, got out of the backseat, and pulled Norris out onto the street. He helped the dazed man sit on the curb.

Then he got back in the car. Joey was already behind the wheel.

"That was nice of you, helping him to his seat," Joey wise-cracked.

"Yes," Benny said. "Wasn't it?"

Joey drove away quickly, but not so quickly as to draw attention to the car.

As the car headed toward the Belt Parkway, Benny asked, "Where'd you get the idea for the ear?"

Joey smiled at him. "Chinatown."

"Chinatown?" Benny asked. "Is that what the tongs do there? I never heard of that."

"No, man," Joey said. "The movie *Chinatown*."

"Huh?"

"That guy in the movie . . . he cuts Jack Nicholson's nose, remember?"

"Yeah," Benny answered. "But what's that got to do with Norris's ear?"

"I cut his ear instead," Joey explained. "Cutting a guy's nose . . . I don't know about that. I mean, that's fuckin' gross."

Benny just laughed. He knew he'd never understand the workings of Joey's mind.

That night was the last time he ever saw Teena. When he got to her apartment, no one answered the door. He tried calling her, but to no avail. She never returned to Pazzo Oeuf. She never formally quit the job. And she never told Benny good-bye, not in any sense.

There were times in the days that followed that he wanted to look for her, maybe even stop by her apartment, but his pride wouldn't let him do that.

Sixteen days later he got a letter from her. In it, she expressed regret at the way she had left. But she said she knew that there was no talking any sense to him of late. At least he might read the letter.

He did. He noticed the envelope it arrived in was postmarked from Delaware. She had probably mailed it on her way home to Virginia.

Benny had mixed feelings about it all. She had been a great girl for a while. He would definitely miss her.

But he knew she would never have fit in *completely* in his life. There was so much she didn't understand, so much she could *never* really understand. Not with her background, not being from where she was from. One had to be raised in this life—or at least near this life—to grasp the reality of it at least a little.

Benny later found someone who *did* understand. He married Deanne Buonocasa a year later.

Her father was a big deal in Atlantic City and was able to get Benny and his associates lots of perks at several of the casinos, sometimes, it seemed, on an hour's notice. He also "supervised" several contracting businesses that operated from Atlantic City to Freehold.

Deanne was wonderful. She was his *regina*, his queen . . . and they made each other laugh. But Teena had been different. Something almost foreign and certainly alluring. And in many ways, Deanne just wasn't in her league. Benny never lost that feeling, not even years later. Not even after his two children were born.

It wasn't that Benny didn't care for his wife. On the contrary, he loved her. It was just that shortly after he got married, he realized just how much he had lost when Teena headed south, not so much, he thought, to get away from him, but to get away from the risks, the dangers, and the contradictions of his lifestyle.

Sorbet

—

A choice of
Granny Smith apple
Coconut
Mango

⚊ Eighth Course: Sorbet ⚊

Benny was growing tired, and he didn't know about the rest of the guys, but he felt he needed a pick-me-up of some kind. In the old days, that "lift" might have come from a line of blow, but snorting the white stuff was a part of Benny's past, not his present.

Today, the lift would come from sorbet, which was something he *still* had a weakness for. He removed three containers from the freezer and placed them on the counter.

Benny peered out into the dining area. A couple of the guys were smoking cigarettes; the others were sitting low in their chairs, which they had pushed away from the table, as if their stomachs needed that extra space. They were all clearly satiated from the meal and could probably use the sugar from the sorbets to help them digest the plentiful food they had eaten.

Benny noticed that Ischia was the only guy on his feet. And he was talking a mile a minute. The rest of the guys just listened to him, up until then not saying very much in response.

"I don't get it," he said. "Am I the only guy here who doesn't know what the hell is going on? We been here for a couple of hours and I, for one, haven't a fucking clue what's supposed to happen."

"Relax, will you?" Di Pietro said. "I don't think any of us knows *exactly* why we're here. But given the situation in the administration, it's not surprising we've been called here tonight."

"What are you talking about?" Ischia responded. "Yeah, there's a shake-up going on at the top, we all know that. But when things settle down—if they haven't already—why not just pass the information through the normal channels? Why this dinner? Why tonight? Why us?"

"Who the fuck knows?" Pally answered. "All I know is that it's better that we're here than *not* here, if you know what I mean."

Benny chose that moment to bring the sorbets into the dining room. "Here you go, gentlemen. This will help cool everyone down."

He placed the three containers on the table. "You've got three flavors of sorbet to choose from: Granny Smith apple, coconut, or mango."

"Jesus Christ," Double A said. "You're like a one-man Baskin-Robbins."

"Baskin-Robbins, my ass," Benny retorted. "You won't get sorbets with this much flavor in any corner ice cream stand."

Ischia returned to his seat. "You seem pretty cool without the sorbets, Benny. You got any information about what's going on?"

Benny answered, "I said before, probably not any more than any of you. The capo is getting ten to twenty, we all know that. And he's getting ten to twenty, give or take, because some rats squealed to the feds. So someone's got to take over. I wouldn't be surprised if we find out who that's going to be before we leave here tonight."

"You think that's all there is to this dinner tonight?" Ischia asked. "It still seems weird to me."

"Yeah?" Benny asked.

"Yeah. Maybe we're all here because this is an easy way to corner one of the rats. You think about that? Maybe one—or more—of us is in deep shit. Maybe they think one of us was involved with one of the rats. Or *is* a rat. Maybe one of us is *going* tonight."

Sapienza sat forward in his chair. "Shut the fuck up, Ischia. Always the cheerful soul, aren't you? Jesus Christ, maybe this, maybe that, maybe, maybe, maybe. Don't you think we all might be thinking the same thing? None of us are fucking rookies here. We know how things go down. But what are you gonna do about it? You wanna leave? Then go. For all the good it'll do ya if you're on the shit list."

The rest of the guys, Benny included, listened to Sapienza, who in many ways was speaking for most of them.

"If your nose is clean, then you got nothing to worry about," Sapienza continued. "As for me, I got a fucking handkerchief in my back pocket. My nose *is* clean. And anyway, just like the rest of you guys, I'm gonna sit tight and see what happens."

Abbazio added, "What else can you do? We just gotta see how this all plays out tonight. I don't think none of us has a crystal ball. All we got is the knowledge of what we've done or haven't done."

Sapienza agreed. "That's it. Double A's right. So unless you've become a problem, Ischia, unless you've become a liability, stop worrying."

"I ain't done anything," Ischia responded angrily.

"No one said you did," Benny answered. "So let's just relax, all of us. Enjoy your sorbet. It'll help chill us all out."

No one said another word. Instead, they took Benny's advice.

Some of them had another cup of espresso with their sorbet. Some didn't. But all of them were suddenly strangely silent, like a group of monks entering into a period of meditation.

Benny returned to the kitchen. He was confident that there was no way he could be considered a rat by anybody, unless someone had been spreading lies about him.

He took a deep breath and, like the guys outside, began a few moments of reflection.

Benny's thoughts turned to the irony of his current situation . . . and the irony of this very evening.

Benny had long given up cocaine, along with lots of other stuff. He really didn't miss it that much, and he knew he was probably a hell of a lot healthier now that he had stopped getting himself all fucked up.

No, he thought, that's one habit he'd never pick up again.

Things were different now.

He had responsibilities; he needed his wits about him at all times; and he needed to set an example for others.

In short, in addition to his restaurant and his position within the syndicate, he had his wife and kids now. Blow's fine when you're single and relatively careless; but the last thing you need when you're older is to lose everything to a nose full of snow. Or to see your kids screwing around with the shit because they know Daddy does it too.

No, it wasn't worth it.

Here he was, leading a pretty successful life, with few cares in the world. He remembered his mother using the phrase "sowing wild oats" when he was kid. She had often used it when discussing some of Benny's boyish behavior with his father. Benny never quite understood the phrase, but he liked the sound of it. It made his wild behavior sound "natural," and it often got him out of a series of punishing whacks from his dad's belt.

There weren't too many wild oats left these days, Benny contemplated. Not that he necessarily missed them. He had two great kids. Joseph was just beginning preschool and loved watching *Sesame Street* on television. His older sister, Vivian, was in kindergarten at Our Lady of Mercy Parochial School and adjusting nicely to her new surroundings. And she was an absolute whiz with the flash cards, especially the addition cards in the arithmetic series.

And then there was his *Regina*. Benny had met Deanne Bounocasa at a gelato café in Park Slope. It had been an awkward meeting.

Benny had bumped into her, causing her dish of gelato to spill all over the sidewalk and, worse, all over one of her shoes.

He apologized profusely, even when she was calling him a goddamn klutz. Eventually, she sat at one of the white cast-iron tables outside the place. Benny had been dazzled by her beauty, so he didn't even mind the name calling. Rather than react in kind, he crossed the street and entered a women's shoe boutique.

A few minutes later, he handed an envelope to the woman.

"Please," was all he said to her when he handed her the envelope.

She was sitting with a girlfriend and hesitated taking the envelope. But her curiosity got the better of her. She opened it and saw the gift certificate for a hundred dollars.

She looked at the slip of paper, then at Benny. Her attitude softened.

"I can't take this," she said to Benny. "Look, I'm sorry I overreacted before. I'm just having a real crappy day."

"Please, then, take it," Benny replied. "It'll make your day that much *less* crappy."

She laughed. "That's really too kind." Then she looked at her girlfriend, whose face said "Are you nuts? Take the damn thing."

"It's not necessary," she insisted.

Benny smiled at her. "It's just a case of 'a shoe for a shoe.'"

"The Bible say that?" she asked, grinning.

"No," he laughed. "*I* say that. My name is Benny Lacoco."

"That's very sweet, Benny."

"It's nothing." He reached into his pocket and handed the woman his business card. "I'd also like to invite both of you ladies to my restaurant sometime. Dinner, of course, will be on the house."

Deanne took the card and read it. Then she looked at Benny and said, "*That* I will *definitely* take you up on."

"I hope you will."

"No question."

"Soon, I hope."

"I hope so, too."

Perhaps foolishly, Benny left then. He hadn't even asked her her name. But a few days later, she showed up at Pazzo Oeuf with her friend. And Benny made them a meal they would never forget.

One thing led to another, and within a few weeks Benny started dating her. They got along tremendously. She was perfect for Benny, a blend of old-fashioned Lynbrook, Long Island, Catholic Italian values and Catholic high-school female rebelliousness and humor. ("Lynbrook!" she once said. "It's Brooklyn *backward*.") She could be sweet, and she could be passionate; she behaved like a lady when it was called for, but also could swear like a truck driver when annoyed; she went to church every Sunday and holy day, but had no qualms about calling Father Flynn, one of her Irish parish priests, a "fucking masher."

In short, she was perfect for Benny.

At least *he* thought so.

And for the most part, he was right.

They were married less than six months after he had spilled the frozen dessert on her foot.

In addition to bringing some sense of love and stability into his life, she also had a civilizing effect on Benny. His extracurricular activities began to diminish rapidly. He hardly spent any time out with the boys. One reason was that he could talk to her as if she were one of the guys. She didn't mind his cursing and coarse language, although Benny always tried to curb that in front of her out of respect. She was streetwise and knew the ways of Benny's associates, and although he didn't tell her *everything* he had been— or currently *was*—involved in, he often felt she understood more than what he told her. In fact, he was often surprised at her insights and her wise suggestions whenever Benny had a "business" problem.

He sometimes wondered if she picked up her business smarts from her father, who he knew had a number of connections in Atlantic City.

Joey was often over to their house for dinner, but even he seemed to sense that most of his and Benny's nights of adventures were over. He too could see the effect Deanne had on Benny. And he was happy for his friend. He could see that she was the ideal woman for Benny: she obviously made him happy and made him feel more secure than he had ever felt.

Deanne's positive effect on Benny became even more obvious once Benny's and Deanne's children were born. Benny cut down on his gambling; not completely, but quite a bit. He was still a sports fanatic, and the gambling just seemed to coexist with the fanaticism.

It wasn't as if she had forced these changes in Benny. On the contrary, they came naturally to him. She—and the kids after they arrived—brought him much happiness, so rarely did he feel the need to go out and blow off steam.

Besides, between the restaurant and his family he rarely had the desire or the energy to go crazy anymore. And although he occasionally spent an evening with his friends in his other family, he was determined to stay out of family dealings that might put his livelihood or especially his family at risk. Of course, he and Joey had become absolute masters of fencing food; that sideline continued and brought them great profit at almost no risk at all.

They had it down to a science.

Aside from the food fencing and the mostly self-controlled gambling, Benny had become as legitimate as he possibly could. He tried to please everyone in the organization and mostly did a good job of it.

But no one in his world was ever *entirely* free of tension. Some guys had long memories, and Benny's past was far from clean.

So after a period of time, when all seemed well, there came a rumbling from above.

The government was coming down hard on the men at the top.

Several of them were guys who had almost always been in Benny's corner. They had helped him become the success he was. And now there was a real good chance that some of them might be serving time in prison.

This caused Benny—like most people in the organization—a great deal of discomfort. There was lots of speculation going on as to who might assume the responsibilities of the family, but no one at Benny's level really knew for sure. And Benny knew that not all of the candidates for the capo opening were supporters of his. He had crossed swords with several people, stepped on others' toes, scammed certain others.

Even those who had usually been in his corner could not be counted on at a time like this. Loyalties shifted with the organization's restructuring, and until the dust settled from the shake-up, everyone was walking on thin ice.

Benny had noticed, for example, that over the past couple of weeks, fewer of his guardians—guys like Ranallo—were visiting the restaurant or even making any contact with him. Benny wondered if he was just becoming paranoid and it was simply a coincidence that this was occurring while the district attorney was witch-hunting and getting headlines or if he were *really* being given the cold shoulder by some of the higher-ups.

He didn't know, though he weighed the situation from every possible angle.

But, like every guy in Il Bambino that night, he was worried about it.

And, he, like the other guys, would just have to wait and find out.

There was nothing else one could do.

Benny popped another couple of Tums into his mouth and let them dissolve.

Dessert

—

Tiramisu with cannoli cream

➤ Ninth Course: Dessert ➤

Man, this looks good, Benny thought, looking at the tiramisu. His stomach was still upset, and he knew he shouldn't even *think* about eating this dessert, but he couldn't resist.

He took a spoonful of the cannoli cream and let the flavor seep into his taste buds. Good, he thought. Very good. Not exactly perfect—maybe a touch too much sugar—but very good.

He washed the mouthful of dessert down with a sip of tepid espresso.

Shit, he thought. I can't wait until this night is over. Then I'll be able to enjoy a meal without wondering if it's my last.

The restaurant phone rang, and Benny answered it. There was a very faint voice on the line, and Benny couldn't understand a word the man was saying. The connection was bad. Or, Benny figured, someone was calling from a cheap cell phone.

He hung up, figuring the person would call back. But whoever it was didn't call again.

A phone chirped in the dining area. Ianello pulled a cell phone from his jacket pocket, flipped it open, and said, "Yep. Ianello here."

He seemed to recognize the caller and rose out of his chair and walked to the front window of the restaurant.

The rest of the guys sat pretending they weren't interested. But some of them clearly were.

They could barely make out Ianello's conversation, but they could see the serious look on his face.

"Must be his old lady," Di Pietro joked.

But at this late hour, this far into the meal, all a couple of the guys could manage were halfhearted smiles at the comment.

Benny too noticed what was going on. Not wanting to miss anything important, he chose this moment to bring out the dessert. He placed the tiramisu in the middle of the table.

"Help yourself, gentlemen," he said, pulling up a chair.

Ianello evidently forgot where he was and yelled, "Are you shitting me? Sixteen years minimum?" into his phone.

Many of the guys shot each other concerned looks. Benny, at least, thought he knew what those words referred to: the capo was getting sent up the river for over a decade and a half. At least, that's what it sounded like.

Double A stared at Benny, and he returned the glance, as if to silently say "Oh, shit!" in unison.

Ianello stepped outside the restaurant to continue his conversation, but after less than a minute, he hurried back inside. Benny thought it must have been the cold that forced him back inside, but when he saw the panicky look on his face, he knew it had to be something else.

But Ianello talked on anyway, though he moved away from the front window and stood behind the bar instead.

"You sure?" he asked. Then he listened to the reply and exclaimed, "I don't get it. How can that be?"

Ischia was the first to pick up a tiramisu.

"Well, if he wants to talk on his phone, he can," he said. "Me? I'm diving into this tiramisu." He bit into it and closed his eyes as if he were approaching nirvana.

Ianello finally shoved his phone back into his pocket. He poured himself a couple of fingers of Chivas and gulped it down. Then he returned to his seat.

"You look like you just spoke to a fucking corpse or something," Sapienza said.

Ianello managed to smile. "No, not exactly," he said, reaching for the tiramisu.

" 'No, not exactly.' That all you gonna say?" Benny asked.

"Yeah, man," Sapienza added. "On a night like this, you're not gonna *share*?"

"How do you know it wasn't a personal call, dickwad?" Ianello asked. "Do you share personal shit with everybody?"

Then Sapienza's phone rang. He casually answered it, without getting up from the table.

"Hello, what's up?"

Sapienza noticed all the guys watching him and made a goofy face, as if he didn't give a damn who was listening.

Then his facial expression changed to one of seriousness.

"No kidding?" he asked. "When was this decided?"

A couple of the guys reached for pastries and started eating them.

"I hardly know him," he said into the phone. A moment later, he said, "Thanks for calling. See ya."

Sapienza put away his phone and ate some of the tiramisu. He said nothing at all.

And it drove the rest of the guys crazy, as he knew it would.

"Fuck, man!" Ianello said. "How about *you* sharing?"

Sapienza swallowed the treat and said, "Sure. I'll trade you. What do you got?"

"What do *you* got?"

"Why should I go first?"

Pally stood up. "Hey, you two mooks! The rest of us ain't got a thing. What's this game all about? Either speak up or shut up."

Benny added, "I think I speak for most of us when I say I'd rather you *speak* up. Particularly if something important is coming down the pike—which it sounds like it is."

"Yeah," Pally urged. "C'mon, spill!"

Ianello finally opened up. "One of my connections at the court said the capo is gonna be found guilty and could get sixteen years. Of course, that's before any appeal or anything. The feds are trying to keep this quiet until tomorrow. But he says the guilty verdict is a sure thing. And he's one of the guards keeping the jury in line."

"That's bad news," Di Pietro said. "Real bad. Who knows who's gonna pick up the reins now."

"I know," Sapienza announced matter-of-factly.

"You do?" Aspromonte said, surprised.

"That's what that call was about."

"So don't keep us in suspense," Benny said. "Who's the new capo?"

"Alfredo Pupillo," Sapienza said. "It was decided last night. Evidently, the men at the top have an even better connection at the courthouse than you do, Ianello, because they got the low-down yesterday."

"Jesus, 'the Hunter,'" Ianello exclaimed.

"What hunter?" Di Pietro said.

"They call Pupillo 'the Hunter,'" Sapienza said. "I don't really know him, though I met him once in Atlantic City."

Benny tried to recall if he knew—or even knew *of*—Pupillo. But he couldn't recall ever hearing of the man.

"So who is he?" Benny asked. "Anybody know him?"

"Yeah, I do," Garguilo said. "He's probably a good choice. He's been involved with many different aspects of family business."

"Like what?" Aspromonte asked. "I know the name, but not much about him."

Garguilo continued. "He's done it all. But he's been heavily involved in the food import business." Garguilo turned to Benny. "I'm surprised you've never had any dealings with him."

Benny shrugged his shoulders. "Me too."

"Especially since he owns a bunch of restaurants. He's got a couple of cousins who run them. Some of them are here in Brooklyn."

"Really?" Benny asked.

"Yeah. Quite a few. Ever hear of Café Bari? His cousin runs that place."

Garguilo smiled at Benny. There was something menacing about that smile. Something that said Garguilo knew something that he could possibly hang over Benny.

And Benny tried not to come undone at the table. But knowing that the new capo was one of the people he had swindled years ago with his food-switch operations made him suddenly nauseous.

He tried to hide the sickly feeling that had come over him.

"I take it you know the new boss?" Benny asked.

"Reasonably well," Garguilo bragged. "I'm sure he'd remember me if we met again."

Double A asked Benny directly, "Hey, man. You look like shit. You okay?"

"Yeah, I'm fine," Benny lied. "Have some more tiramisu."

Ianello stood up. Sweat was dripping off his face. "Christ, it's hot in here."

He walked over to the bar. "I need a fucking drink."

But when he got to the bar, instead of pouring himself one, he just stared out the window, clearly looking for something . . . or someone.

"Shit!" he muttered.

"What's the matter with you?" Di Pietro asked.

"He's gone."

"Who's gone?" Double A asked.

"Nobody."

"Nobody, my ass," Di Pietro continued. "When you were at the window before, and outside, you acted like you saw a fucking ghost. You practically came *running* back inside."

Benny sat forward and addressed the group. "I saw him earlier too. And it was no ghost. It was Big O."

"Big O?" Ischia repeated frantically. "What's he doing here?"

Nobody answered. Nobody had to. They all knew the Big O was no social butterfly. He showed up when he was needed, when there was some job to be done that no one else wanted to do or when the bosses wanted a job done in a particularly unpleasant manner. The only other time the Big O could be seen was if he were on bodyguard detail.

But there didn't seem to be anyone else outside who he might be protecting.

The restaurant phone rang and interrupted the morose, temporary silence. Some of the guys looked at each other with curious or concerned looks on their faces; others drank their espresso or ate the tiramisu, trying to seem nonchalant.

"I better answer it," Benny said, getting up from the table.

He walked behind the bar and picked up the receiver.

"Hello," he said.

Then he just listened. For several minutes he didn't say a word. He just listened to the voice on the other end.

Finally, he hung up the phone. Then he walked back to the table.

"So?" Double A asked.

"It was Ranallo," Benny replied. "He said no one is to leave until we get word or someone from up above shows up."

"What's the deal with that?" Ianello commented.

"Who knows," Benny said. "But something's going down. That's for sure."

"He say who might show up?" Aspromonte inquired.

"No. Just said we should stay put."

"Someone's already here," Ianello said nervously. "Or have you already forgotten our friend outside?"

"I thought you said he was gone?" Garguilo asked. "So relax."

"Relax?" Pally repeated. "That word and the Big O don't belong in the same sentence."

Di Pietro took a mouthful of tiramisu. "There's nothing any of us can do, so we might as well make the best of it. Can't let these pastries go to waste."

The rest of the guys just looked at him, speechless.

"What?" he asked. "What did I say? The tiramisu? Hell, it ain't poison; it's fucking incredible, though. Might as well eat. Anyhow, the longer I'm sitting here tonight, the more I'm getting the impression that if the brass wanted somebody gone, they would have had Benny slip us some fucking rat poison or something in the food. That didn't happen, so there must be a reason."

No one answered Di Pietro.

But Benny thought about what he had said.

The bosses *could have* gone that way, even though Benny had never killed anyone, least of all with his cooking. At least not intentionally.

Could it be, Benny asked himself, that *he* was tonight's target? Did the new capo have a grudge against him after all? Benny had, after all, been selling some of his people substandard food and making a tidy profit from doing it. And still was, for that matter.

But Benny got that thought out of his head as quickly as it had come. Why would the boss set up this elaborate dinner—prepared by Benny—and then off him after it? Why make him work so hard? Just to bust his balls before whacking him?

It didn't make sense. At least he didn't think so.

"Benny," Double A called out. "You okay?"

Benny snapped out of his meditation. "Yeah, just tired, that's all."

"I'd fuckin' love to know who else cooperated with the FBI," Garguilo said. "There were tapes of phone calls up the ass in court."

"I thought the papers said Joe Costa was wearing the wire," Di Pietro said. "The fucking rat."

"Yeah, but Costa wasn't working alone," Garguilo continued. "He had to have had accomplices."

There was contemplative silence for a moment; then Garguilo turned to Benny and asked, "You and Costa were pretty tight, weren't you, Benny?"

Benny was taken aback both by the question, and especially by the *tone* of the question.

"He's eaten at my place a few times," Benny replied matter-of-factly. "Then again, so have you. And I wouldn't exactly call us *tight*, would you?"

Garguilo started to reply, but cut himself off. "Whatever," he said instead.

Double A sat forward. "You know, you guys are too fucking much."

"What are you talking about?" Garguilo asked.

"I'll tell you *exactly* what I mean. First, Pally's got a beef with Benny. Now *you're* on him like lint on a sweater. What the hell is going on here? The fucking guy's made this fantastic meal, and everybody dumps on him."

"What are you?" Garguilo asked, "His fuckin' guardian angel?"

Benny stood up. "That's enough. I don't *need* any guardian angel, though I appreciate Double A's intentions." Then he faced Garguilo directly. "I also don't need *your* bullshit. I don't give a shit if you know the new capo or you're his best friend or you're kissing his ass."

Di Pietro said, "Hey, Benny, take it easy. We're just talking here, that's all."

"Is that so?" Benny replied. "Just talking? Garguilo here seems to be trying to intimidate me, like he knows something. But we all know he doesn't know shit. He just likes to sound like a big man."

Garguilo stood up also. "Fuck you, Benny. We'll see what's what soon enough."

"Yeah," Benny said. "We will."

Then he grabbed the now empty tray of tiramisu and headed for the kitchen. Over his shoulder he said to the men, "Help yourself to an aperitif and a cigar, everybody." He did his best to sound like he didn't give a damn about anything.

From inside the kitchen Benny heard Garguilo say to Double A, "If I were you, I'd be careful who you side with."

Then he heard Double A reply, "Fine. But you aren't me."

Some of the other guys joined in the exchange, but the various voices all blurred together in Benny's mind. He threw the tray on a counter, put the palms of his hands on the countertop, and leaned over. For a moment, he thought he was going to be sick.

But the wave of nausea passed quickly. Benny stood upright and wiped a towel against his brow, which was lined with beads of sweat.

He didn't know where he stood anymore. The digs between him and Pally earlier in the evening were insignificant, and, more importantly, were over. But this sudden eruption from Garguilo was something entirely different. This wasn't just personalities clashing; this was beyond that.

This was Garguilo hinting that he knew what was coming. Whether he actually knew or not was anybody's guess. But the jabs he had been throwing Benny's way were starting to get on Benny's nerves.

And although Benny had never even met the new capo, he *had* done business with him. Then there was that matter of De Cresenzo, the capo's cousin, who ran Café Bari. And Benny *did* know Joe Costa, and liked him a lot. That was long before Costa turned traitor.

At least Benny hoped it was.

This was all getting to Benny now. Could it be that I'm the one to be iced? Benny wondered for a moment.

Jesus!

Oppido was somewhere around outside. He must be here to pop someone, Benny knew.

Jesus Christ!

It *can't* be me, Benny thought. I'm no big guy in the organization. They're after whoever cooperated with the feds, not some guy like me who sold them second-rate olive oil. Why would they waste their time with little crap when the capo was going away? It just didn't make sense. Not at all.

Benny felt better. He had reasoned it all out. *He* couldn't be the target. It had to be one of the other guys.

He wiped his forehead again, took a deep breath, and told himself to keep cool, no matter what. He knew he could. He'd been doing it all night.

Everything would be fine.

Everything *was* fine.

Then Benny turned to get some fresh espresso and saw a figure standing in the far corner of the kitchen.

He was wearing a hat and a long coat. And from under the coat the figure slowly drew out a sawed-off shotgun. Just enough so that Benny could see it.

Benny couldn't really see the man's face that well, since the brim of his hat shadowed the upper half of his face. But he didn't have to see it any more than he needed to know how the man had gotten in to the restaurant.

He knew who he was.

The Big O.

And when the man put his forefinger across his lips to signal that Benny should remain silent, Benny had no trouble following that direction.

He was startled speechless. And he couldn't take his eyes off the man's lupara, his customized sawed-off shotgun.

Cigars and Cordials

—

*A selection including the best stogies
Havana has to offer*

Last Course: "The Just Desserts"

The Big O stood motionless, staring at Benny. But it wasn't the stare or the sawed-off shotgun that unnerved Benny.

It was the smirk on his face. Or at least what Benny could see of it, since the upper part of his face was darkened by the shadow of the man's hat.

The dining room was filling up with cigar smoke, and the Sambuca, anisette, schnapps, and other spirits were being poured and consumed by the guys. Benny silently prayed that no one would do anything to rile Oppido. Just someone entering the kitchen might be enough to trigger Big O into some sort of violent action.

Then the gunman broke the silence in the kitchen.

In a surprisingly soft voice he said, "You got any Manhattan Special in here?"

Benny wasn't sure he heard correctly. "You mean the soda?"

"Yeah," Big O said. "The coffee soda."

"I don't think so. There might be some at the bar."

Big O just stood still.

"Do you want me to check?" Benny asked nervously.

Big O thought about it for a moment, then answered, "Yeah. I really feel like drinking one now. "

Benny moved slowly and cautiously toward the door to the dining room. He couldn't believe that at this particular moment a man with a shotgun was asking for a soft drink.

"Yo," Big O softly called out before Benny reached the door. "Don't do nothin' stupid. Go out, check the bar, and come right back. I'll be watchin' the whole time. Don't let on that I'm here. If I even think you're doing anything stupid, I step in. You understand what I'm tellin' you?"

Benny nodded agreement.

Big O waved the gun toward the door, signaling that Benny could leave the kitchen. Which he did.

Benny hoped he could keep himself together and not do anything to piss Big O off. He walked directly to the bar, saying nothing to the assembled guys. He walked behind the bar, opened the door of the small refrigerator, and looked inside.

No Manhattan Special.

He closed the door and headed back to the kitchen. Surprisingly, none of the guys said a word to him.

Benny reentered the kitchen. Big O was standing in the exact same spot. But he had put the gun down. It was on a counter next to him, within easy reach.

"Sorry," Benny said. "No Manhattan Special."

Big O removed his hat and placed it next to the gun on the counter. "That's too bad. I really have a craving for one."

Benny faced him not knowing how to respond. Or what to do.

"Is there something you want me to do?" he asked.

Big O looked at his watch, then simply answered, "Very soon. Any minute now."

Then both Benny and Oppido heard someone in the dining room say, "Holy shit! Here comes company."

Big O grabbed his gun and moved toward the window looking out on the dining room. But he didn't look through it himself.

"You tell me what's happening," he instructed Benny. "And don't act like a jerk. You give me away and . . . just stay cool."

Sapienza headed to the front door and opened it. Three men entered.

Benny didn't recognize one of them. He was elderly and tall and thin and had a bushy mustache. He looked like one of the old-school guys, the type they referred to as Mustache Petes.

The second man was very young, probably no more than twenty-five. He entered the restaurant, saying nothing at all and never once taking his hands out of his overcoat pockets. Benny had seen him around, but didn't really know him.

The third man was Ranallo. He looked tired and somewhat older than the last time Benny had seen him.

"So?" Big O asked, practically whispering in Benny's ear.

"Three men," Benny said. "One of them is Ranallo. I don't know the other two."

Big O quickly peered through the window, then pulled back.

Benny noticed he was smiling.

Benny wondered just what that grin meant. He also thought about Ranallo's presence here right now. That might be a sign that Benny was safe. After all, Ranallo was a major part of helping Benny become who he was.

But then Benny recalled the relationship Ranallo had had with others. At least twice that Benny knew about Ranallo had had to do in a couple of ex-associates. Lacerra, for one. And the guy in Flatbush—Brandi—who had the seafood allergy. Big O poked

Benny gently in the side with the sawed-off shotgun. The touch of it against Benny's body made the chef twitch.

"You go out there and sit down," the gunman said quietly. "Don't even think about letting on to anyone that I'm here. You got that?"

Benny nodded.

"Go," Big O said. "Nice and easy."

Benny entered the dining room and moved to its center, where he knew Oppido could see that he *wasn't* doing anything stupid. Sweat was beginning to pour down his face.

Ranallo saw him and asked, "Benny, my friend, you're sweating up a storm. You must be working hard in that hot kitchen."

"It *is* hot in there," he answered. It wasn't until the words had left his mouth that he realized their ambiguity.

Ranallo addressed all the guests. "Everybody sit down." He waved his hand toward the table, still covered with glasses, ashtrays, and a couple of plates. "C'mon, everybody take a seat. We've got some business to attend to."

Benny tried to study Ranallo's face as he looked at each of the men in attendance. But it was impossible to tell anything from his demeanor. The man was a pro, and if he had business with someone in particular, Benny couldn't tell who that might be.

Finally, all the men, Benny and Ranallo included, pulled up chairs and sat down. Ranallo positioned himself at the head of the table, and Benny sat somewhere toward the middle, between Sapienza and Aspromonte.

The two men who had come with Ranallo didn't sit at all. The older man lingered behind the bar, and the younger man stood by the front door of the restaurant. His hands were *still* in his pockets.

"We have some talking to do, gentlemen," Ranallo began. "Before we start, would anyone want a drink or anything?"

No one seemed to want anything, so Ranallo nodded and continued.

"Okay. As you can probably guess, there's been a change at the top and at several levels below that. I cannot stand here and guarantee that *all* the changes have been made. A big wave causes lots of little ones. An earthquake often has many aftershocks. That's the best way I can explain it right now."

Ranallo reached for a pitcher of water and poured himself a glass. During this minute, many of the men shifted positions in their seats. Most of them were clearly on edge.

After taking a sip, Ranallo went on. "You've heard by now, I'm sure, that there were several canaries singing to the feds in court. We are fully aware of who these rats are."

"Pardon me for interrupting," Garguilo said, "but aside from those snitches in federal custody at the moment, do we have everyone else involved in the federal probe identified?"

"Are you asking me if we know who they all are?" Ranallo asked.

"Yeah."

"We think so, let me put it that way. Of course, there are always a few snakes hiding under the rocks. But we'll get them."

"Thank you," Garguilo said, sitting back in his chair, content.

Benny knew Garguilo had asked that question to intimidate him. But it didn't completely work. Benny knew he *hadn't* had anything to do with the feds; furthermore, it was pretty clear from the way Ranallo was talking that *someone else* had. Perhaps someone who was here tonight.

"If I may continue, gentlemen," Ranallo went on, "there are

obviously going to be some further changes made in the structure of our family. Some of you will benefit from these changes, I am certain. However, before we continue, I want you all to reassure me that none of you has been part of this ongoing conspiracy, this airing of dirty laundry, that is now going on in the courts and in the press. You know what I mean."

Everyone sat silently. Glances passed from man to man. And to Ranallo.

"No one has anything to say?" Ranallo asked. "No one has anything to add? Or to confess?"

Again there was silence.

"Mr. Sapienza," Ranallo said, "You have nothing to say?"

Sapienza leaned forward. "No. Nothing."

Ranallo turned to Double A. "Mr. Abbazio?"

Double A unfolded his arms and sat up straight. "No."

Ranallo next turned to Benny. "Mr. Lacoco?"

Benny thought his heart would explode, it was pounding so hard. But he managed to say, "Nothing."

Ranallo took another sip of water. Then he said, "I won't go around the table like a schoolteacher trying to identify a trouble-making student. But I will say this: If any of you knows something, this is not the time to keep it to yourself. The honor and very structure of the organization are at stake. If you are guilty of something, we will eventually find out and you will be dealt with severely. If you are guilty and speak up now, there is a chance that the punishment will not be so severe. If you know something involving anyone here tonight that must be revealed to preserve the structure of the organization, you must speak up. It will not be considered ratting out an associate. It will not be regarded as a betrayal in any way. It will be for the good of the family. Understand?"

Again, none of the men responded. This time, though, hardly any of them made eye contact with Ranallo.

"Very well, then," Ranallo continued. "Let me illustrate to you exactly what I mean by severe punishment."

He turned to the kitchen and gestured with his hand.

The door to the kitchen opened and Big O stepped into the room. All eyes turned to the imposing figure. And all those eyes saw the gun that still protruded from the overcoat he was wearing.

Big O approached the table and stood directly behind Ranallo. It was impossible to look at Ranallo and not see the hulking, daunting figure behind him.

The man behind the bar stayed where he was, as did the younger man by the door.

Clearly, Benny thought, the moment of truth was arriving. Seeing the Big O and the other two men standing at their positions reminded Benny of the climactic, three-way gunfight at the conclusion of *The Good, the Bad, and the Ugly.*

Only these three would not be shooting at each other.

And this was no movie.

"I ask you all for the last time," Ranallo said. "Now or never."

Garguilo said, "I have something to say."

Ranallo nodded to him. "Go on."

"I feel I must say something about one of us present here, though it breaks my heart to do so."

"Speak freely," Ranallo said.

"I have it from a most reliable source that one of us assembled here *did* cooperate with federal agents."

"And who would that be?" Ranallo asked, deep concern in his voice.

Garguilo didn't answer right away. Instead, he seemed to be overcome with emotion.

"You must speak up," Ranallo demanded. "We are a family. The guilty must be identified and dealt with. Even if that person is one of our brothers."

Garguilo composed himself. "I regret to inform you that I am referring to . . . Benny Lacoco."

Benny had felt it coming before Garguilo even got the words out. The son of a bitch was a good actor, he'd give him that. All that choked-back emotion.

But he was also a lying scumbag.

"That's bullshit!" Benny said, leaning forward over the table.

Big O stepped over to the left and positioned himself directly behind Benny's chair.

"This isn't possible," Double A said aloud.

"But it is," Garguilo affirmed.

Ranallo raised his hand and the talking stopped. He stared at Benny and didn't seem to be able to hide the disgust he was feeling.

Then he turned back to Garguilo. "And who is this reliable source that gave you this information?"

"I don't know that I should say," Garguilo said.

Ranallo smiled. "Of course, I appreciate your, uh, discretion, but you have made a most serious accusation against one of us. You *must* reveal to us the source of this information. Now!"

Garguilo's face suddenly lit up. "I was told this by the new capo himself. I am honored that he trusted me enough to personally share this information, as disheartening as it is, with me."

Ranallo looked down at the table. "I see."

That's it? Benny wondered. That's all Ranallo is going to say? He's going to take the word of that lying pig without saying anything else?

"The capo told you this himself?" Ranallo asked.

"Yes," Garguilo answered. "As I am certain you must already know. Just as I am certain you already knew that Benny has betrayed us. Isn't that, after all, why you . . ." he looked across the table at Big O, then continued, ". . . and your associates are here?"

Ranallo smiled sardonically and nodded his head. "Yes, I too have received information from the capo."

Benny couldn't take it anymore. "But it's a lie. I've been set up."

Big O pulled out the lupara and pointed it against the back of Benny's head. Benny stopped talking. The other guys stiffened in their seats.

Ranallo told Benny to shut up, then turned back to Garguilo.

"You are indeed fortunate to be so close to the new capo," he said,

Garguilo smiled. "Yes. I know most of his immediate family. And I am the godfather of one of his cousin's sons."

"How nice for you. And you say that you received this information about Lacoco from the capo himself?"

"Yes. As I am sure you received it yourself. After all, wasn't this evening set up to trap Lacoco? I mean, it is sheer genius on the part of the new capo, isn't it? Keep the traitor busy in the kitchen?"

"Quite ingenious, yes."

Benny couldn't take it anymore. "This is all bullshit," he said.

Big O pushed the barrels of the shotgun against the skin of the back of Benny's neck.

Ranallo continued. "The new capo apparently has let you into his inner circle and feels you are one of his honored confidants. You should see this as a very great honor."

Garguilo nodded and said, "Yes, a *very* great honor. And our new capo, Alfredo Pupillo, is a very great man. May God bless him always."

"Yes," Ranallo agreed, "especially now."

"Yes, on the day of his appointment."

Ranallo shook his head in disagreement. "That isn't exactly what I meant."

"It isn't?"

"No. You see, Pupillo isn't the capo. Mario Cottafavi is."

Garguilo turned to Sapienza. "But just an hour ago, Sapienza got a phone call saying that Pupillo . . ."

Sapienza leaned forward on the table. "I guess I lied," he said curtly.

Ranallo continued. "Pupillo is not only *not* capo, he's dead. His term as capo lasted for less than eight hours."

"That isn't possible," Garguilo said, noticeably shaken.

"But it is," Ranallo asserted. "It was decided that no one likes a rat, and that no one wants a rat to be capo."

"What?" Garguilo asked.

"You know very well, even without the big words and niceties," Ranallo said.

Then he signaled Big O, and the steel barrels that were pressed against Benny's neck were suddenly lifted over his head. The gun now pointed directly at Garguilo.

The young man who had arrived with Ranallo moved away from his position at the front door of the restaurant and wandered over to the table. The older man behind the bar took the younger man's position as guard at the entrance.

"You were part of the conspiracy, Garguilo," Ranallo explained. "Pupillo himself fed information and phone tapes to several lesser rats—yourself included—who then passed them to the feds. All to get himself ready to take over as capo."

"That's a lie," Garguilo said angrily.

"Did he cut a deal with the feds? Maybe. Anyhow, too many people saw through his plan. And the bastard thought he'd bring down pretty much everyone else he didn't care for. Even Benny here. You would have let him die, wouldn't you, Garguilo? Even though he had nothing to do with the feds. All that, just to cover your own ass. Make it look like you cornered all the rats."

Garguilo panicked and tried to run. But before he could completely get out of his seat, the young man moved behind Garguilo and wound a garrote around Garguilo's throat.

The men sitting next to Garguilo slid their chairs out of the way as much as they could. A couple of the guys turned their eyes away from the violence.

Benny watched, however. He saw Garguilo's face turn purple, saw his eyes bulge and go glassy, saw his tongue come out between his open lips as if trying to lap up some oxygen and bring it into his lungs, as his neck began to bleed from the open seam caused by the garrote. He heard the gagging sounds coming from the liar's gullet.

Then Garguilo slumped back into his chair. The young man untied the garrote from Garguilo's neck. The dead man's face fell over onto the table. The young man put the garrote back in his pocket and stood still, watching attentively.

Benny leaned back in his chair. The back of his head momentarily leaned against Big O's chest. Realizing that, Benny again leaned forward.

Then he felt a hand grasp his shoulder.

Benny looked up at Oppido.

"It's alright," Big O said. Benny thought the big man was actually trying to smile.

"Gentlemen," Ranallo said, "you can all relax now. I'm so very glad that my friend Mr. Oppido here did not have to use that cannon of his. God knows those things make *so* much noise. I am sorry we had to set up this big trap to catch this little rat."

He looked at Oppido and asked, "Can I impose on you further to get this mess out of here?" He pointed to Garguilo.

Big O slipped the sawed-off shotgun into some sort of holster he had under his coat and walked around the table. The men sitting next to Garguilo kept their chairs away from the dead man. Big O grabbed Garguilo by the back of the collar and sat him upright in the chair. Then, in one fluid motion, he slid the chair back, bent down, and carefully threw Garguilo over his shoulder.

"Thank you," Ranallo said.

Big O gave a slight nod in return. Then he walked into the kitchen with the body across his shoulder.

That was the last Benny saw of Big O.

Ranallo called to the older man behind the bar. "Bring over a couple of bottles, will you, Dario? I'm sure our friends here can use a drink or two."

The older man brought over a bottle of Johnnie Walker Black and one of Jack Daniel's. Ranallo passed the bottles around, and the guys drank up.

Eventually, the talk among them became more relaxed. The shock of the evening was slowly wearing off, and all of the guests at this dinner were feeling very relieved.

Even the young man who had executed Garguilo sat down and joined the others at the table. He even took his hands out of his pockets. And Ranallo introduced him to the others as Chris Anzelone, adding that he was "my nephew from Roma. His older brother, Giovanni, is a priest in the Vatican."

Then, when Ranallo announced that any of the men could leave whenever they wanted, several took the opportunity by paying their respects to Ranallo, complimenting Benny on the feast he had prepared, and exiting immediately.

But Pally stayed. He lit a cigar and asked, "So when are the girls coming?"

None of the guys could figure out if he was kidding or not.

But Ranallo answered, "Sorry, my friend. You just had a huge meal and a bit of excitement. If you need excitement of *that* sort, you'll have to provide your own tonight."

Eventually, several others drifted out of the restaurant. They too said the proper respectful words to Ranallo and thanked Benny for the great dinner. Then only Ranallo, his two accomplices, Double A and Sapienza remained.

Then Sapienza said he would be leaving too.

"Thank you for your help tonight," Ranallo said to him. "Your telling him Pupillo was still capo was instrumental in getting Garguilo to give himself away. I knew calling *you* before was the right choice."

"But if he hadn't pointed the finger at Benny?" Sapienza asked.

Ranallo smiled. "We would have got him some other time.

We were fairly certain—due to his ties to Pupillo—that he was involved with the feds' probe. This little—what should we call it?—dinner theater tonight just sealed his fate."

Benny sat back in the chair. He was thoroughly exhausted. But he was glad he was feeling exhausted. He was glad he was feeling *anything*.

Sapienza said his good-byes, and Double A announced he was leaving too. Benny stood up and embraced both Sapienza and Abbazio.

"Take care of yourself, man," Benny whispered in Double A's ear.

"Go fuck yourself!" Abbazio said in reply. Both men laughed. Even on a night like this, Double A refused to pass up the chance to say *that* to Benny.

After they had gone, only Benny, Ranallo, and his two associates remained. Benny just stood near the table. He was too restless to sit anymore. He felt like a massive weight had been lifted from his shoulders.

Ranallo stood up and hugged Benny. Then he said, "I'm sorry to have put you through this tonight, Benny. But it was unavoidable. We needed to have Garguilo hang himself with his own words."

"I understand," Benny said. "But couldn't you have tipped your mitt or something?"

Ranallo shook his head, then smiled. "No. I didn't want to risk giving you any signal that would have screwed this all up."

"I can appreciate that," Benny responded. "I'm just glad it's over. And I hope you never for one moment thought I would have violated *omertà*."

"Not for a minute," Ranallo confirmed. "You are one of my prizes, Benny. I know you would never violate the code."

Then he smiled. "Maybe even if you *had*, I would have tried to arrange a pass for you. Chefs like you are gifts from God, and they are to be protected. My only regret is having missed this feast tonight."

Benny said, "I can fix you up something now if you'd like."

"No, no," Ranallo answered. "Some other time. You've done enough all day. In fact, why don't you go home when we leave, which will be in a minute. I'll send some people over to clean up for you, both out here and in the kitchen."

"That would be great," Benny said. "Thank you, Mr. Ranallo."

The younger man helped Ranallo on with his coat. Ranallo embraced Benny and patted him on the back.

Then Ranallo and company left.

Benny looked around.

He was alone.

He wasn't sure what he was feeling. Part of him wanted to laugh; another part wanted to cry. Yet another part wanted to drink the remaining half-fifth of Johnnie Walker.

He did none of those things.

Instead, he headed for the kitchen, put on his coat and said aloud, "Jesus goddamn Christ!"

After turning out the lights and locking the front door of the restaurant, Benny crossed the avenue and entered Cobbler's. The place was still crowded for so late on a weeknight.

Then he spotted Joey sitting on a stool halfway down the long mahogany bar. Benny walked up to him and patted him on the back.

"Hey, man!" Joey said. "Glad to see you."

"You don't know *how* fucking glad I am to see *you*," Benny replied.

"So can you talk about it or what?" Joey asked.

"I can, but not now, man."

The bartender came over—the same bartender who had served Benny earlier in the evening.

"You're back."

"Just like I said," Benny replied, ordering drinks for himself and Joey.

The jukebox kicked on. Someone had played Pat Benatar's "Hit Me with Your Best Shot." Benny found himself tapping his right foot to the song as he gulped in one swallow the scotch the bartender had brought.

Joey drank down his scotch too. "Hey, Benny, you mind if we split? I didn't think you'd be here so late. It's almost three o'clock. I can hardly keep my damn eyes open."

"No problem," Benny answered. "Let's go."

He threw a twenty-dollar bill on the bar and the pair walked out of Cobbler's.

"Oh shit, I just remembered," Joey said.

"Remembered what?"

"What the hell is calcados?"

"What?"

"What the hell is calcados?"

"What is it?" Benny repeated. "Is this a joke or something?"

"No, I'm serious."

"Calcados?" Benny thought about it for a minute, then said, "Oh, you mean calvados, the apple brandy?"

"Got me," Joey replied. "It *does* come in a liquor bottle."

"Yeah, it's a French apple brandy. Very expensive. Some chefs use it in desserts and other recipes. Why do you ask?"

Joey's face broke into a big smile. "Because, Benny, I got twenty-seven cases of this calvados in my garage. I sorta found them . . . you know, in a warehouse. I thought maybe we could move them."

Benny just looked blankly at Joey. "No," he said. "I can't deal with this right now. Good night, Joey."

Joey shrugged his shoulders. "Okay, just thought you'd like to know. Good night."

They headed for their cars.

Then Benny turned and called out to Joey. "Call me tomorrow about fencing that brandy, just not too early."

Joey said, "You got it."

Then Benny got into his car, cranked up his radio, and headed for home.

He was going to give his wife and his kids an extra kiss good night.

ENHANCE YOUR BOOK CLUB

1. Bring a copy of Mariah Stewart's first novel in the Hudson Sisters series, *The Last Chance Matinee*, to your book group's meeting. Are there any passages you or your fellow members may have highlighted that you want to revisit?

2. Consider reading Mary Alice Monroe's Low-country Summer series or Kristy Woodson Harvey's Peachtree Bluff series for your next book. Do you see any similarities between the writing styles, the characters, or the locations? Is there anything else you'd like to consider discussing?

3. Des admits that her favorite romantic movie is *Pride and Prejudice*, but she says she does not have a favorite version. As a group, consider reading the original novel for your next book club pick, or watch one of the more recent versions of *Pride and Prejudice*. Is there a particular cinematic version that your group likes best?